Lily wasn't used to someone worrying about her simply because they cared.

Be careful, a voice whispered to her. *No one is to be trusted—not even Jon.*

Confused and frustrated, she became aware of a shadow falling over her eyes. It was slight, but clear: something was covering her eye the instant before her lid came down.

"Jon, what's going on? What's happening?" She started to shake.

Then she felt it, rising along her spine, from tail-that-wasn't to whiskers-that-weren't. A sense of connection, of power, of strength that was alien and yet entirely hers...

"Lily!"

"Oh." She gasped, her world reeling. "Oh goddess..."

Lily felt her knees give way, and she collapsed in Jon's arms.

Books by Anna Leonard

Silhouette Nocturne
The Night Serpent #48

ANNA LEONARD

is the nom de paranormal for fantasy/horror writer Laura Anne Gilman, who grew up wondering why none of the characters in her favorite gothic novels ever seemed to know a damn thing about ghosts, vampires or how to run in high heels. She is delighted that the newest generation of heroines has a much better grasp on things. "Anna" lives in New York City, where either nothing or everything is paranormal....

She can be reached via
http://www.sff.net/people/lauraanne.gilman/ or
http://cosanostradamus.blogspot.com/.

THE NIGHT
SERPENT

ANNA LEONARD

Silhouette Books

nocturne™

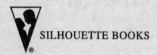

SILHOUETTE BOOKS

ISBN-13: 978-0-373-61795-1
ISBN-10:   0-373-61795-X

THE NIGHT SERPENT

Copyright © 2008 by Laura Anne Gilman

www.silhouettenocturne.com

Printed in U.S.A.

Dear Reader,

Growing up, I used to love reading those "gothic" novels filled with things that went bump—or grrr—in the night. They fascinated me, and I started looking for other "spooky" myths, reading voraciously in the horror and fantasy fields as well. I was delighted when paranormals made a comeback—and even more delighted to see that we'd gotten a generation of heroines who feel that same fascination with the supernatural, and love to be a little spooked!

So join me, please, in a world very much like our own—a world that might even be our own—where love and betrayal are often hand in hand, second chances must be earned and the past can never be outrun....

Anna Leonard

For KRAD and TO

May your life together be filled with love,
joy, satisfaction and success.

Eight times before she had traveled this dream-road; traveled, and been lost. Eight times before, the same sensations haunted her sleep. The feel of the sun's intense heat between her shoulder blades, the heavy slip of linen across her shoulders, the sweat of fear down her neck. The sound of scorn in his voice as he cast her aside. Most of all, the low vibrating purr, the gentle rumble that chilled her, made her eyes scrunch closed and pray to a vengeful goddess that mercy would at last be granted her....

And the Voice, echoing forever in dream-memory. "As you destroyed, so must you repair. Until then, child-of-mine-no-longer, walk these sands as one forgotten, never to be judged worthy, never to rest—"

"Mother, please..." She wasn't sure what she was asking for. Forgiveness? Absolution? A chance to explain, to make an excuse?

No matter. It did not matter. It never mattered.

Eight times she bowed her head to the inevitable, knowing there was no excuse she could make, and no explanation she might offer that would wash the blood from her hands. Her birth and position would save her from public humiliation and shame, but inside, in her ka, *she would always know. Always remember.*

"Mother, I am sorry. My children, I am so very sorry...."

A soft touch against her skin, fur stroking skin. She flinched from the comfort, welcoming the pain that followed. Agony, the sharp downward stroke of betrayal, over and over and over again. Then... darkness.

When she woke, she would remember none of it. She would forget.

Eight times, she always forgot.

This was nine.

Chapter 1

Lily Malkin undid the barrette holding her hair out of her face. The thick black curls slid past her shoulders, and she reached up to run her fingers against her scalp, feeling herself relax. The headache that had haunted her all morning, residue from her usual insomnia, eased a little more.

"Mrrrup?" A tiny paw batted against her knee, demanding attention, and the chance to claw those curls.

"Hello, Rai." Lily scooped the tiny silver tabby up in one hand, easily keeping the needle-tiny claws away from her hair. The kitten complained, and she soothed it by stroking the soft head until the outraged expression was replaced by heavy lids and a gentle purr.

Lily could almost feel her own eyelids lowering in

response. Kitty nap-vibes, the other shelter volunteers called it: the sincere conviction that everything in the world could be made better by stopping to nap in the sun. Oh, if only that were true. She raised the kitten higher and touched her nose to the little pink one. "There you go. Life's not so bad. And it will only get better for you now, I promise."

The kitten, secure in her grip, kneaded its claws sleepily against her skin, but didn't otherwise respond. Lily only wished that her problems were that easily solved. Never a particularly good sleeper, she had been averaging less than four hours a night for the past month, and it was taking its toll.

Madness takes its toll. Please have exact change ready. The old joke was even less funny now than it had been in college, she thought. At least then, she had exams and a social life to blame for her exhaustion. Now… Now there were only dreams that she couldn't remember, and a sense hanging over her that there was something, somewhere, she needed to do. Something important.

The sad truth of the matter was that there wasn't anything really important in her life. Not in the way that niggling dream was telling her.

Maybe it was time to go back to therapy. Or visit a psychic. Or start taking sleeping pills. Something.

Rai dug tiny needle-claws into her hand, informing her that the petting had stopped, and why had the petting stopped? An obedient human, Lily stroked the downy head again, until the claws relaxed.

A deep voice above her, filled with laughter, broke

her concentration on the tiny animal. "You, Lily Malkin, are a miracle."

"Me?" Surprise made her voice rise, making the word even more of a question, but she kept her attention focused on the kitten, afraid to startle it and ruin the progress they had made. She felt like many things right now, but none of them were miraculous.

"You, yeah. Three years ago, just looking at a cat made you break into a cold sweat. Now?" Ronnie, the director of the Felidae No-Kill shelter, sat down on the floor next to Lily, where a pair of inquisitive kittens immediately pounced on her. The two women were in the middle of the "socialization" room, a space filled with climbing trees, catnip mice and rope nets—and almost a dozen cats and kittens in various stages of sociability. "And now? Now you're our very own 'cat whisperer.'"

Lily made a face. She hated that nickname, and "cat talker" and "cat lady" and all the other terms the other volunteers and media people had stuck on her. But there didn't seem to be any way to get rid of it, now.

It was ironic, really. Despite her last name having a traditional, if unfortunate connection to cats, from the time she was a child being around cats had made her uneasy both physically and emotionally. Physically, she got dizzy, sweaty palmed and nauseated. Emotionally…she had nightmares triggered by something as simple as hearing a cat meow.

Despite that, cats still seemed drawn to her, climbing in her lap and weaving in and out of her legs at the slightest chance.

"It's because you're scared and sit so still," people had told her, as though that made it all right. And, in truth, she had always—from a distance—admired cats, with their easy strides and poised gracefulness, and the way they could curl up, nose, toes and tail, and be instantly comfortable anywhere. But the unease kept growing, to the point where she could not visit homes of friends with cats, or even watch a cat-food commercial on television without changing the channel.

Over the years, that unease had transferred to people, too. She watched them the same way she watched cats, wondering what they wanted from her, what they expected, and when their demands would overwhelm and consume her.

It wasn't rational, but nothing Lily had read about phobias over the years indicated that rational thought was involved.

When she had moved to Newfield three years before, it had been with the plan to make a new start after the collapse of yet another relationship, her fourth since graduating college. This time, she had told herself, she would not make the same mistakes. New town. New start. Except that she didn't know how to begin.

Her problems had started with cats—she thought maybe she could start there, and work her way up to people. A helpful therapist and a lot of pep talks had gotten her to the door of the Felidae No-Kill shelter, meaning simply to volunteer in the front office, maybe greet people when they came in, help maintain their Web site, or…

It hadn't quite worked out that way. The fact that she

was where she was, the ranking volunteer with the most responsibility…

Maybe Ronnie was right. Some days even she could barely remember the person she had been the first time she set foot in the doorway two and a half years ago; shaky, sweaty and ready to pass out at the sight of the first inquiring whisker. It had been that much of a change.

With cats, anyway. Lily still had trouble with really connecting to people beyond casual friendships and working relationships.

But she didn't speak cat, or have any kind of supernatural connection with them, the way some people seemed to think. Cats were just easy to understand. The things they wanted were simple: scratching, and feeding, and a warm place to sleep and to be left alone when they were enjoying all those things.

People? People always wanted more, and they never seemed able to just come right out and ask.

"I think this guy's going to be ready to adopt soon," was all she said, lifting the tabby and putting him next to a large orange tom named Willikers, who promptly started grooming the kitten. "And he'd be fine in a house with older cats. Maybe even a dog, if he was used to cats." Talking about cats—and their adoption chances—was easier than talking about herself.

"I'll note that on his chart," Ronnie said, accepting the change of subject. "In the meanwhile, you should try to scrape off some of that cat hair. There's someone here to see you."

"Me?" Again, her voice rose, this time almost to a

squeak. Maybe that was what she needed to work on next, not sounding so anxious when people noticed her.

Her boss nodded, absently petting the calico she had chosen. "Your faithful mechanical Mountie just stomped in, looking for you."

Oh, Lily thought. Then, uh-oh. She knew what that meant.

Resigned, Lily stood up and brushed without much hope at the denim of her jeans. She had quickly learned not to wear wool or corduroy at the shelter, but cat hair could stick to anything, and with the multicolored cats they were currently housing, there wasn't a color you could wear that wouldn't show the inevitably shed fur. Giving up, she gave her cotton sweater a tug, ran her fingers through her hair to get the overlong curls off her face and went out of the glass-enclosed socialization room and into the lobby.

Two men were waiting for her. One was an older man, craggy-faced, wearing casual slacks, a button-down shirt and a gray blazer that had seen better years.

"Detective Petrosian." Formal in the presence of a stranger, for all that they had known each other for two years now.

Aggie—Augustus—Petrosian looked up, and Lily knew for certain that she wasn't going to want to hear what he had to say. It was going to be worse than her usual calls, which were more along the lines of removing a litter of kittens from the inner walls of a building that was being torn down, or getting someone's illegal pet—last month it had been a half-grown ocelot—out of an apartment without anyone getting bitten. When he showed up with those sorts of problems, Aggie never looked as grim as he did right now.

"Lily. Thank you."

She smiled at him. He always said that, as though she was going to hide in the backroom and pretend he wasn't there.

"Lily Malkin, this—" and he indicated the man next to him "—is Special Agent Jon T. Patrick. He's with the feds. Visiting us here in the burbs to help out on a case."

"Patrick" as a surname sounded as Irish as it got. This guy, Lily thought immediately, wasn't even remotely Irish; not unless they had packed up and colonized somewhere more exotic when history wasn't looking. Intense black eyes looked out from deep-set sockets. Those rather amazing eyes, emphasized by a thick, short cap of black-and-gray curls above and the high brace of cheekbones below, were all you saw at first. Lips were thin, ears ordinary and skin a soft golden tan that gave her the urge—briefly—to lean forward and find out what he smelled like. Sandalwood, she thought, without knowing what sandalwood actually smelled like.

Oh. Also, oh. If she were a shallow woman, her mouth would be watering right about now.

All right, so she was a shallow woman on occasion. It wasn't a crime.

He looked her up and down and then directly in the eyes, and the intensity of that gaze felt as though he was undressing her almost casually, as though he had the right to do so. That kind of arrogance pissed her off, so she stared back at him, daring him to continue. At least she had been discreet in her observation.

You're not that *hot, pal,* she thought, now annoyed by how quickly she had responded to him. It hadn't been *that* long since she'd… All right, maybe it had. That was still no reason to react like a tabby in heat.

Detective Petrosian finished the introductions quickly, as though he sensed the undercurrents. "Agent Patrick, this is Lily Malkin. Lily's our local cat expert."

Her lips quirked at Aggie's words, despite her irritation. Between him and Ronnie… She wasn't any kind of expert, really, just cheaper and easier to get hold of than any specialist they could afford to hire, even if one were available. Newfield was a small city, as cities went, and they had an equally small budget to cover a lot of far more urgent needs.

Agent Patrick didn't seem too impressed, by either her or her credentials or his surroundings. His gaze was still on her, but it had become a polite, indifferent look, and his mouth—too thin, she decided, and not to her taste—was held flat, as though he was biting back a comment.

So much for her federal rating, she thought. He probably preferred athletic blondes. Not that he was her type either—she preferred her dates to be a little less obviously high-maintenance.

Agent Patrick did dress well, though. Or maybe that was in contrast to Aggie's familiarly rumpled self—the gray suit and white shirt was probably issued in bulk at FBI headquarters, but it fit Agent Patrick's tall but solid form, and his tie was not the usual power red, but a dark gray-on-gray pattern that was both stylish and surprisingly soothing.

The agent hadn't looked away from her yet, despite his disapproval, and Lily felt the back of her neck prickle under that steady regard. He needed to blink, at least. If she had been one of her four-legged charges, she might have hissed and arched her back to look more fearsome and drive him away.

"Lil." Petrosian was speaking again. "Lily, I'm sorry, but I gotta ask you to do something ugly."

Her attention left the fed and narrowed to the expression on Aggie's face: regretful, but determined. She had been right. Whatever it was, it was going to be bad, especially if a federal agent was along. Lily had no idea what she might be able to help with, at that level, but she trusted Aggie Petrosian as much as she trusted anyone. He was, maybe, the only person she truly did trust. He asked of her only what he asked, and nothing more. No hidden agendas waiting in the shadows. He had always been up front with her. Like a cat. And because of that, if he needed her to do something, she would do it. It was that simple.

Even if it meant being in the company of this Agent Rude-stare Patrick.

"All right."

Special Agent Jon T. Patrick wasn't usually so obvious when he checked someone out; contrary to popular opinion, the bureau did install some couth and control in their people. And his mother would have slapped him over the sofa if he was rude to a woman. But from the way this woman—Ms. Lily Malkin—was shying away from him, he'd been both obvious and obnoxious about it.

Nice move, smooth guy, he thought in disgust. But she had taken him totally by surprise.

When the detective had collected him at the airport, Patrick had expected that they would go directly to the site, since it was still relatively fresh. Instead, as he loaded his bags into the back of the unmarked sedan, Petrosian had informed him that they were going to make a stop along the way, to pick up another consultant.

Patrick bristled at being called a consultant—if he wanted to, he could have used his credentials to argue for the lead in this investigation, and the detective knew it—but instead he merely nodded and let his gaze rest on the scenery. Newfield wasn't much to look at; the airport was just outside city limits, and they were passing the usual patch of warehouses, followed by blue-collar neighborhoods of two- and three-family houses, then into the city itself. He thought they might stop at the university, or maybe the police department.

The last thing he had expected was to find himself in the lobby of a run-down animal shelter, being introduced to a black-haired, peach-skinned pocket Venus wearing faded blue jeans and a black V-neck sweater that made you want to run a finger down the crevice…

He jerked his attention back to the woman's face as Petrosian asked her to accompany them. Her skin was smooth, with wide-set hazel eyes, a sweetly rounded face and a chin that was just blunt enough to keep her from being cute. Malkin. An old, useless bit of information filtered through his magpie memory and into recall; an old slang term, meaning a slatternly woman, or a scarecrow. It also, ironically, had been used to mean both rabbit and cat. She had the nervous posture of a rabbit, but the sleek lines of a cat.

And Lily? Lilies had long necks, like…

Patrick shut that line of thought down, aware that his brain could sometimes go off on totally random tangents. Work related: that was good. Libido related? Less so. Keep it official. Keep it on business.

The detective didn't explain to Ms. Malkin what was up when he made his request, and she didn't ask for details, indicating that they had done things like this before.

Patrick was reassured by that, the familiarity and the trust, both. Consultants, in his experience, usually asked too many questions up front. That prejudiced their read of the site before they even got there, making their evaluations useless. So she was not only sexy, but smart. And, apparently, from the coolness in her hazel eyes while she looked at him, wanting nothing to do with one special agent.

Blew that before you even knew you were doing anything, didn't you, Jon T.? He could hear his mother scolding him, across seven states and two time zones. *How will you ever meet a nice girl if you scare them all off?*

Yeah, yeah, Mom, I know, he told the voice. *Very* smooth. I'm a moron.

Not that it mattered. He was here on business. The case—ordinary enough on the surface—might be nothing more than a garden-variety cat killer howling at the moon, which he could leave for the locals. Or this guy might in fact be an embryonic serial killer just starting his progression: if so, finding what triggered him would support his own personal theory, and stopping the guy would help cement his standing in the bureau. A federal officer's career was all about reputation: making it, and keeping it.

It was never good to alienate a local expert, however dubious her standing, this early on, though. Petrosian thought enough of her insight to make a special trip to ask for her assistance, and the cop had come across as a pragmatic, by-the-book guy.

Patrick rubbed his chin thoughtfully. Well, if he suddenly needed to borrow the brain inside that lovely casing, then he'd pull out the professional charm and make her forget that she'd ever thought badly of him. The fact that she rang his bell would just make that job pleasant, rather than a chore.

"Let me get my coat, I'll be right back."

"Patrick." The cop got his attention with a thick, stubby finger waved under the agent's nose. "Don't underestimate her," Petrosian warned. "She may look like a little girl, but she's smart. And tough."

Patrick raised his eyebrows at Petrosian's wording. The last thing he would ever describe that woman as was "little girl."

"Aggie. You driving?" She was back, a denim jacket pulled over her sweater. Clearly, the chill air outside didn't bother her at all. Spring in New England, ha. He was already homesick for D.C.'s milder weather.

"Yeah. I'll bring you back after, okay?" Petrosian was already herding them out the door. That was fine by Patrick—the crime scene wasn't getting any fresher while they stood here. The sooner he got to it, the sooner he could determine if he had any business being here at all.

The dark green sedan slid through traffic, heading away from the downtown area into more residential blocks. Petrosian left the radio muted to a quiet squalk and their cat lady didn't seem inclined to talk, so Patrick took advantage of the time, sitting in the backseat, to go over his notes and compare them to the official file on this incident. There wasn't much in the update Petrosian had given him at the airport, and he closed it without having made any more progress than he had since getting the original material via the local bureau office the night before. The information was too slim: he needed to see the site himself, form his own impressions. That was why he was here: his skill was in transforming direct observation into a working and workable theory. Someone else's observations, with their inevitable biases, were useless to him.

"Please, don't let anyone have fubar'd the scene."

"What?" Petrosian raised his eyes to the rearview mirror to look back at him.

"Nothing," he said, gesturing at the files in explanation. Thankfully, Petrosian just nodded and went back to his driving. Bad form to tell your host that you expect his men to be incompetent. No, Patrick thought ruefully, he was not getting off on the right foot with anyone here so far.

Ten minutes later, they parked outside a small storefront, a single-story corner convenience store in a neighborhood of small, neatly maintained houses with neatly, if unimaginatively, tended lawns and a grade school down the block. There were two squad cars out front, but no yellow tape to be seen anywhere. Ms. Malkin got out of the car and waited for Petrosian, who gestured her toward the front door. She nodded once, her body language changing from uncertain to aggressive, and moved up the walkway. Another thing to like, Patrick noted: she took possession of her scene like a pro. It took them a year to hammer that into cadets at the academy, and some of them never learned how to do it.

Lily had been aware, the entire ride, of Agent Patrick's presence directly behind her. Oh, he hadn't done anything, hadn't said anything, but she could practically feel him looming behind her.

All right, "looming" was overstating it. He was sitting normally, going through an official-looking file of papers and photos, barely even glancing up as Petrosian took corners too quickly, only once muttering something she didn't quite catch. But when he did look up, she felt his gaze like a physical touch, as soft as a cat's tail flick and just as unmistakable. It wasn't unpleasant, exactly…but it made her uncomfortable.

He made her uncomfortable. And it wasn't just because he was good looking. Or even because he was arrogant. Lily had seen better and worse examples before, both on her job and in dealing with the cops and the press. But there was something about this guy that was putting her on edge.

Or maybe it was this…whatever it was that Aggie had called her out for, and Agent Patrick was just catching the fallout. She wished that she had asked for more detail before agreeing, but...

It didn't matter, not with regard to Agent Attitude. Either way, it wasn't as though she was going to have to deal with him for long; she could put up with the arrogance and just enjoy the eye candy while it lasted.

When they arrived, she got out of the car before Aggie had even finished parking, looking around curiously. She had lived in Newfield for three years, but she didn't know this neighborhood. It seemed a little rundown, but reasonably safe. Although, she admitted, that might have had something to do with the noticeable police presence on the street.

"Up here," the detective said, waving her toward the storefront. She swallowed hard and went inside, passing a uniformed officer in the doorway.

There was no warning: one moment she was moving forward, and the next she was knocked back on her heels, a full-body slap.

Aggie had said it was ugly. *Ugly* wasn't the word for it. Lily stopped just inside the doorway and blanched, the back of her hand pressing against her mouth while she swallowed, hard, and tried not to breathe.

"Oh God."

The inside of the front room was splattered in red; walls, counters and empty glass-fronted display cases. In a photograph it might have looked like paint; the smell told the real story. Some atavistic sense in the back of her brain told her what the tinge in the air was, and what the spray, by default, had to be: blood, with the undercurrent of meat starting to go bad.

But the floor was what caught her attention: a cleared space in the middle of the room, the pale green linoleum tiles covered with a black cloth about four feet square. On the cloth, seven still, limp forms were arranged in an odd-shaped circle, nose to tail.

Cats.

And, without warning, she was back in the echoes of a dream. *Cats, sprawled as though basking in the sun. Only there was no sun, and their heads turned wrongly, their tails stilled, their voices silent.... A shadow rose behind her; despair and terror flooded her throat....*

"Oh, the poor moggies," she heard Agent Patrick say behind her, and the faint flash of not-quite-a-dream shattered. Her mouth was dry, her skin clammy. Where had it come from, that flash, that overwhelming, painful visual? It wasn't a memory, nothing she had ever seen. She would remember something that horrible. But where had it come from, then? Television, maybe, or something she had read?

It didn't matter, she decided, trying to shove it away. The here and now was disturbing enough.

"Who did this to you, little ones?" she heard the agent ask, obviously speaking to the cats, and the discomfort she had felt in the agent's presence earlier was diluted by an instant and unexpected kinship with him. Arrogant as he might be, there was real sympathy in his voice. They weren't just animals to him—they were victims.

"I'm going to need photos from every angle," he barked to Aggie, taking command of the scene as if it had been deeded to him. Clearly, no matter how much he might have felt for them, he was all business now.

The arrogance that had annoyed her earlier was re-assuring now. Attitude was much more appealing when matched with clear competence.

Lily took a shallow breath, and regretted it. The bodies weren't fresh. More than a day, from the smell, but not much longer, or it would be worse. She thought it would, anyway. Actually, she had no idea, and wasn't able—or willing—to turn around and ask Aggie for an answer.

"You were the one who found the bodies?" Patrick was now asking the young cop nearest him, who nodded. The man—a boy, really—looked as ill as she felt.

Intellectually, Lily knew that people did things like this. The first year she worked at the shelter, around Halloween, she'd been asked to help with two black cats that had been tortured by a couple of wannabe Satanists, to see if the cats could be used to identify and hopefully convict their abusers. It had been a slow news week, and the media had gotten hold of the story. The shot of her leaving the scene with one of the cats clinging to her, his triangular head hidden in her hair, had run every time they touched on the story. That had been what started the "cat talker" nickname. The press had hounded her for a week afterward, even though she refused to give any interviews or sound bytes. Petrosian had sworn to run interference with the press from then on.

Lily didn't like being in the spotlight. It made her nervous, the same way the unblinking scrutiny of cats once had, as though someone was judging her, finding her lacking, unworthy. Not the way Agent Patrick had, but deeper down, where it mattered. Where you couldn't avoid it. Connection, a therapist had told her once. She wasn't good at maintaining connections. The responsibility made her nervous, made her wonder how she had failed, even when she knew that she hadn't, couldn't possibly have.

But nobody was watching her now. Even Aggie had turned away, joining Agent Patrick in talking to the cops on the scene, giving her a moment to regain self-control.

"Your people have already been through?" Agent Patrick, his voice still and intense again, as though the lapse into emotion had been a—well, a lapse.

"Last night, yeah, when we made the discovery of this new source." Aggie's gravelly rumble was soothing by comparison. "Everything's been documented and swabbed, but since no humans were involved, we left the scene itself intact, as per your request. As soon as you're done here, we'll bag and tag it."

Lily stood over the circle, wondering what she was doing there. Normally, at a scene, there was a live cat present, of some breed or another, that she could observe and interact with. Normally there was something she could *do*. Now, all she could do was to take in the details, look at the still, unmoving, cold bodies, and wonder who could have done such a thing.

God have mercy on them, the poor innocent beasts, she thought. She wasn't much for religion—going to church had always left her feeling more empty than fulfilled, and her brief foray into Buddhism during college wasn't much better, but there had to be *someone* who looked after those so ill used....

She swallowed hard against the surge of emotion, willing herself into professional behavior. Thankfully, some coolly analytical portion of her brain came forward, sorting the scene into dry facts, something she could process, the way she handled numbers at her day job at the bank. All right then. Aggie wanted her here for some reason. She knew cats. So she would study the cats.

Seven bodies, all spotted tabbies, their silver, gray and white coats covered with black thumbprint-size spots, tails striped with wide black marks. Young, male. Not at their full growth yet, they weren't, with tails too long for their bodies and ears too large for their heads. There was a slice across each throat, a puddle of red underneath where each one had bled out. Where had the blood on the walls come from, then? How much blood was in a single cat, multiplied by seven?

No, don't go there. Keep the thoughts all clinical, detached, distanced, and unreal. Safe. Like counting out money, entering numbers. Important but not emotional. Not anything that could make her chest hurt for the horror of it. Lily was good at being practical, at making the world make sense, especially when it didn't. She only wished she'd had more sleep last night.

The headache was back, sneaking up like a bully with bad intent, and Lily wished she had taken her own car, which had painkillers stashed in the glove compartment. She reached up to rub the ache between her eyes, allowing her concentration to slip.

That was a mistake: the separate details clicked into

a whole picture, the smell and texture and reality of it slamming into her. *Wrongwrongwrongwrong!* A sheen of red to match the blood on the floor and walls rose over her vision, and her hands shook until she clenched them together. Someone had done this to cats—to *kittens.*

The headache was swamped, disappearing under the onrush of rage. Anyone—any*thing*—that could do that needed to be stopped. Punished.

She felt someone coming up behind her, the heavy tread and swish of wool uniform slacks telling her who it was even before the smell of stale cigarette smoke that hung around him reached her, mingling with the smell of blood and meat and, oddly, settling her stomach before she even realized that it was upset.

"What do you need me to do?" she asked Petrosian, not taking her eyes off the scene. If he heard the rage in her voice, either he had been counting on it, or he didn't want to call attention to it, because he didn't flinch or make any movement to try to soothe her.

"I don't know," he said instead. "I'm hoping you can tell me. Tell us what's going on. What happened here."

She looked over her shoulder, then looked back at the cats, and then up at the ceiling, which, she noted now, had been painted black. The paint looked oddly flat, under the fluorescent lights, as though it had been meant to reflect softer, kinder lights. None of the blood had reached that high, she noted. "Other than animal abuse?"

"That much we got. But that's Patrick's problem, what he's here to study. What I want you to take a look at is back here." Petrosian's thick-fingered hand came down on her shoulder, steering her past the grisly tableau, the only apology for putting her through this that he could give her, the only one she would accept.

Out of the corner of her eye she saw Agent Patrick kneeling by the bodies, pulling on a pair of latex gloves before reaching out to touch one of the kittens gently.

He looked up and met her gaze. A spark seemed to jump between them, invisible electricity that she felt through the palms of her hands, running like a ribbon of warmth all the way to her feet.

He looked away first, and in another place, another time, she might have felt a flush of feminine triumph. But not here.

There was another room behind the first one, and that was where the smell was coming from. Ten mesh cages, each one with a water dish—most dry—and spilled dry kibble. A small plastic box in each, half filled with uncleaned litter.

"Nobody touched anything once we found it. How many cats, Lily? How many cats were here? Tell me what this guy was doing with them."

Usually she had to listen to the cat's vocalizations, watch its body language, before she got a read on the situation, on how it had been treated. Not this time. This time it came out of the empty space, swarming her, almost knocking her over.

Crowded. Anticipation. Fear. Hunger. Lust.

Even without the cats, she could feel the emotion still in the room, could almost hear them meowing, scratching at the wires of their cages, scratching at the metal floors, the rasping of their tongues as they tried to keep fur clean and claws sharp…. Not a bad dream. Not something she could block, ignore or forget.

She gagged at the strength of the knowledge, forcing the words out carefully. "More than ten. More than… there were kittens here. Litters."

That was the smell she had picked up, even over the blood and shit. Pheromones. The scent of a female cat in heat. The thought made her ill, where the killings had only made her angry.

"He was breeding them. This wasn't just storage, it was a cattery."

"Go, do your thing," Petrosian had said to him when they got out of the car. The cop hadn't said it rudely, or mockingly, the way some did; more along the lines of "you do your thing and I'll do my more productive thing." Profiling was still looked at sideways and suspiciously by a lot of folk, especially outside the agency. Hell, Patrick knew that he occupied a strange sort of niche within the FBI hierarchy itself: he had a master's in psychology, but he had never been interested in profiling, preferring to play a more active role in chasing down criminals. He might have had a very traditional career; fieldwork landing him in a desk job leading him all the way to retirement and possibly a teaching job after that, except that during his second year in the field he had discovered in himself an odd fascination for—and affinity for solving—a particular kind of crime, specifically animal mutilations, and the criminals who perpetrated them. Those acts, along with a few others, often heralded the beginning career of a serial killer.

A profiler got into the head of an unsub—bureauspeak for an unknown subject of an investigation. He tried to feel where they were going, mentally and emotionally, and sense how close they were to breaking out to human victims. Patrick was less interested in what went on in their heads than in the end result; the instinctive reaction response to that internal stimulus. His skill might have ended up simply as a side talent, except that he was very very good at finding those patterns, even where none seemed to exist. And so, whenever a case with certain elements—domestic animals, ritualistic injury—came up in the reports, the agency tapped him to immediately take a look. Catch an unsub when he was still targeting animals, and save human lives later.

That was the theory, anyway. There was no quantitative proof either way. It could all be hand-waving and luck.

Patrick had, in self-defense, come up with his own theories about sociopaths and the making thereof. Forget the psychology, the biochemistry, the sociology. Jon Patrick was a believer in *intent*. Not that someone chose to be a stone-cold killer, but that they always had a trigger, something to make all the parts come together from where they lay latent in every single human being.

He focused on the ritual aspect rather than the actual violence—violence was universal in the end, while the steps chosen to get there were individual. Identify a strain of ritual, and determine where that particular mind might go, criminally. Find the pattern break the pattern and prevent a killer from being born.

The problem was that, without enough distinct data points to prove or disprove his ideas, he couldn't get anyone to take them seriously. And being taken seriously was what Agent Jon T. Patrick was all about. Being taken seriously, and getting serious results.

He was damn good at his job, though, and even if his ideas were unsubstantiated, his results were getting him some notice at higher levels; the bureau cared less about theory than they did about getting results they could use. The suits back in D.C. were marking him as a player of note, and Patrick had goals above and beyond being a field agent with nightmare memories and a passable retirement package at the end. Ambition, to him, wasn't a dirty word.

His career, if he didn't screw up, was looking good. It was all good.

This, though…this wasn't good. He made a circuit of the scene, aware of the technician taking additional photographs and jotting down measurements, observations and verified facts. Good—he would need the daylight shots, too. He knelt beside the small, still bodies, careful not to disturb the black cloth or the blood splatter around it, and pulled a pair of latex gloves from a pocket, sliding them onto his hands His last girlfriend had referred to them as fingercondoms. He had been amused by that: a pity that had been the extent of her sense of humor.

"Poor moggies," he said again, reaching out to touch one of the bodies. The flesh was firm even in death, meat and muscle over the ribs. The cats hadn't been abused before being killed. Small mercies. But that put a different spin on the scene, and his unsub. Usually animals were tortured before they were killed. It was all about power in most cases. Power, control, authority. To kill animals that, although helpless, were undamaged, especially in such a methodical, almost ritualistic manner? All it lacked was an athame—a ritual knife—and some candles, and the press would be screaming black magic.

He didn't believe in magic, black, white, pink or polka-dot. He did believe in the power of belief, though. Believe something, and you could take power from it. Believe in it strongly enough, and it took power over *you.*

Normal people with normal emotions didn't kill small cute cuddly animals. This killer was bent at best, and possibly a textbook sociopath, working his way up to more of a challenge.

Despite the violence inherent in the act, though, Patrick got the feeling that this guy wasn't acting out of unformed rage or irrational fear. He wasn't striking out in any desperate attempt to be heard, or regain control or any of the usual textbook profiles. There was a cooler, more rational mind behind this. A mind with a list, maybe, or a plan.

Intent. What was his intent? What triggered him to take cats, care for them, kill them, arrange them this way and then just leave them here?

"Is this guy just your everyday boring psychonutter," he said, sitting back on his heels and looking at the bodies. "Or is there something else going on? And if so, what? Where is he coming from, that this is a logical progression?"

What he wouldn't give to be able to talk to this guy,

to unpack his brain and see where the wires went and which ones were crossed….

A noise behind him made him look away, up and toward the door to the backroom. Petrosian and the woman—Malkin—were coming back. The cop looked a little grim around the mouth, issuing soft-voiced directions to the painfully young uniform who had been first on the scene. Ms. Malkin—he tried to read her expression, and failed utterly. It was as though a stone wall had come up, leaving him no opening to see through. Even his charm might not be enough to win her back, if he needed her help with this case.

Then she looked up, and he almost recoiled. Even under the fluorescent lights overhead, there was no mistaking the fury in those wide-set eyes. He had never bought into that whole cliché of flashing or sparkling eyes—eyes were just bits of meat and veins, and they did not shoot anything except glares.

But he would have sworn an oath that Ms. Lily Malkin's hazel eyes filled with dangerous green sparks as she stared at the dead cats under his hand.

It was scary. It was also, he admitted to himself, pretty damn hot.

Chapter 2

Lily had gone outside to get some fresh air. She was waiting there, watching the cops canvassing the neighborhood, when Patrick and Petrosian finally came out. It was close to 4:00 p.m., and dusk was falling. She loved winter, but getting to it… Autumn just depressed her. She shivered, crossing her arms over her chest, less from the evening chill than the inner one. The spark of attraction that had warmed her earlier was long gone.

She tilted her head, looking for the first evening star. It was an old habit from her childhood, stargazing. But no matter how many times she looked, however much she read about constellations, the sky never seemed quite right to her, the ancient drawings in the sky never familiar. She kept looking, hoping that one night the patterns would suddenly make sense to her. They never did. They didn't tonight.

"Sorry, took longer than I expected," Petrosian said, breaking her concentration. "I just need you to give a report, and then you're done. Okay?"

Normally she did whatever they needed her to do, and went home, or took the cats involved to the shelter for processing. This was different. Everything about this was different. Knowing that there were people who were cruel, who could do things like that; it was different actually seeing it. Experiencing it.

It made her ingrained distrust of the world suddenly seem like a good idea, not a handicap.

"Lily?" Petrosian was watching her, his careworn face filled with regret. "I'm sorry. I needed you to go in without any knowledge beforehand…." He had apologized more to her tonight than in all the time they had known each other.

Aggie and his daughter, Jenny, had adopted three cats from the shelter, two since she had worked there. Max, a red tabby, and Wilma, a calico shorthair. He had been the one to suggest her name when the department first needed a cat expert and had been her contact person ever since then. He knew more about her, simply through observation, than even members of her own family. He knew what he had asked her to do.

"Yeah. Me, too. Sorry, I mean." Only she wasn't sorry. She was angry. But without knowing where to direct that anger, it weighed her down and simply made her tired. And cold. The crisp night air seemed to cut into her bones. "It's okay, Aggie." No, it wasn't.

It was very much not okay. But it wasn't Augustus Petrosian's fault. "Let's go."

There were two police stations in Newfield, one uptown and one down. There was a substation, Lily knew, that was closer, but Petrosian took them to the uptown station instead. Agent Patrick excused himself the moment they arrived to make a phone call, and the detective handed her over to a sketch artist, a tall, rounded woman with a ready smile and ink stains on her fingers and a smudge on her freckled snub nose that made her look too young to be working in the police department. She introduced herself as Julia, and brought Lily to a square table in a small room off the main hallway, out of the flow of traffic. There wasn't a door to the room, but the chatter, slams and creaks of station activity flowed around them, turning into a babble of white noise.

"All right. Detective Petrosian says you've got a scene for me?"

"I thought sketch artists did faces?" Lily didn't really care, she felt too exhausted by what she had seen to worry about anything else, but it made for conversation. Conversation was easier than thinking. Kinder than thinking.

"Mostly, yeah. But we do whatever it takes to close a case, same as everyone else here. So. What've you got for me?"

So much for not thinking. Worse, they wanted her to *remember.*

Lily sat down at the table, in the chair Julia indi-

cated, and closed her eyes. She had thought—had
hoped—that once away from the site, the visual would
fade. But the moment she shut out the distractions
around her, it came back, and she began to describe it,
slowly, trying to hit as many details as possible. Something stuck in her throat as she talked, and hurt, like it
was hard-edged and heavy, and the more she talked, the
worse it became.

"All right. I think I've got it."

Julia's voice seemed to come from far away, down
a long tunnel. Lily opened her eyes, resurfacing into
the noise and bustle of the police station. Julia was putting down her pencils and Agent Patrick was standing
behind her, looking down at the sketch with a fascinated expression.

"This is what you saw?"

Lily frowned, confused by his question. He had been
there, why was he so surprised? Julia turned the pad
around and slid it across the table so that she could see.
It was the cattery, but not abandoned now. Each cage
was filled with four or five shadowy bodies: adult cats
in some and kittens in others, almost all of them with
dappled coats. Dishes overflowed with dried kibble,
and water was slopped carelessly onto the counters.
There was a figure in the middle of the room, but so
roughly drawn that it was impossible to determine if it
was male or female. Tall and lean: hunched over
slightly as though expecting a blow.

"You saw this?" Agent Patrick asked again, his voice
intent on the question. She responded almost unwillingly to the urgency in his voice.

"No. Not really. The room was empty." He knew that. He had been there, too.

"But you described it. Every detail." His voice wasn't exactly doubting, but it was skeptical that she could have managed it without prior knowledge, something she wasn't telling them.

Lily was too shocked to take offense. She looked at Julia, who nodded. "I don't add anything the witness doesn't tell me, not until we go to the next stage. Everything there's what you told me to put down."

Lily looked at the sheet again, and a sense of familiarity moved through her. Yes. This was what the room looked like. The cats, restless and calling each other. The figure moving among them, taking them away and—sometimes—bringing them back. The smells of food and urine against the stainless steel of the cages, the hint of antiseptic…

There was no way she could know any of that. But she did. As much as she knew anything that happened today. She could even pick out the shadowed forms of the cats that had been selected for death, there, in the far cage, segregated from the others.

"You psychic?" Agent Patrick's voice had evened out, not making judgments in a way they had to teach in the academy. "Humor the crazy person, and then disarm them" would have been the motto of that class, no doubt. He probably got an A. It should have rankled, but looking at the sketches, Lily just felt tired. He was only doing his job, and part of that job was to doubt everything.

"No." She looked at him, then down at the drawing

again. "It was just how everything was laid out. This is the only way it could have been."

That didn't satisfy him, she could feel it in his gaze, in the way he looked at her, and then at the sketch, and then at her again. He didn't accuse her of lying, but he didn't quite believe her, either.

She couldn't explain it. She couldn't prove it was true, what she described. But it was.

"All spotted cats," Julia noted.

"Yes." She was certain of that, too.

"Tabbies, mostly. The slaughtered animals here had white paws. How common is that?" Patrick was staring intently at the drawing, clearly trying to work something out in his mind. He had put aside the question of her accuracy, and was working with the available evidence, no matter how dubious.

"What, mitting?" Lily said. "It's pretty common, no matter what the coat's color. Especially if he'd been breeding them—there weren't that many queens in the room, so the gene pool was small."

"Queens?" Julia asked.

"Breeding females," Patrick said, surprising Lily with his knowledge. "A queen can breed every four months, anywhere from three to seven kittens in a litter."

For a moment, Lily felt that spark running between the two of them again, a spark that had nothing to do with his dark eyes or undeniably masculine appeal— or his interest in her. A cat person. Or at least, one who had done his homework. That tied in to the feeling she had gotten from him at the scene: that he saw more than statistics and splatter.

Aggie had said the agent focused on animal abuse cases, something about him psychoanalyzing killers the way they did on TV shows. But that made her wonder—why was an FBI agent, a profiler, investigating something like this? What made cats important enough to interest a federal agency?

Suddenly Lily felt herself deflate. Of course he was interested in her, a cat person. It was part of his job. Well, that was what she was here for; to help him, however she could, to catch this guy.

"He—whoever was doing this—didn't have more than three queens in the room, from the size of the cages. But a lot of kittens. You think he was trying to breed for a particular color?" Lily had never really thought about the genetic side of cats before; all she knew about different colors was what was more popular among adopters.

He shrugged. "I'm not ruling out any theories at this point."

"And what is that point, exactly?" *Why are you here?* she meant.

Julia touched the sheet, the motion drawing their attention. "I'm sorry. I need to run this over to the detective. Lily, if you want to wait, I can make sure an officer—"

"I'll make sure Ms. Malkin gets home safely," Patrick said, cutting Julia off, and then smiling at her to soften his rudeness. "I'd like to ask her a few more questions first, if we can use this desk?"

"Yeah, sure." Julia seemed flustered at being the focus of his attention, which Lily thought was odd, but then the artist gathered herself back into professional mode. "Will you want a copy of the sketch?"

"That would be wonderful, thank you."

Lily watched Julia's slender white hands gather up her pencils and the sketch, then disappear into the swirl of noise around them. Somehow, it seemed distant from her, even now. She had known about the queens, the female cats. How? How *could* she have known anything she had told Julia to draw? Extrapolation from a few cages and a smell could only go so far, but—

But, stop, she told herself, feeling the old, familiar, *unwanted* distress crawling back. *Stop.* Breathe, Lily. Breathe in through the mouth, out through the nose. Breathe, and be still. A lifetime of dealing with panic attacks—she might not need the technique on a daily basis anymore, but it still did the job. Her anxiety level dropped until she felt as if she could manage again.

"Why is the FBI investigating this?" she asked, once her breathing was under control.

"We have varied interests," Patrick said, sliding into Julia's seat with a grace that belonged to a more slender man. If he noticed her momentary distress, he didn't mention it. "Why do they call you the cat talker?"

She shook her head, too worn-out to be either angry or amused at his evasion or the appearance of her hated nickname. "Who told you that?"

"One of the uniforms. Said you could talk to anything feline, get it to do what you wanted."

"Anyone who said that knows nothing about cats." Lily looked up finally, and in doing so was caught again by Agent Patrick's gaze. Dark, yes, and intense, yes, and totally focused entirely on her, in a scary-nice sort of way. Oh. So that was what he'd done to the sketch artist. You could get lost in those eyes, just watching them watch you. It made her nervous. Something, hell *everything* about him was making her nervous. Like he thought she was one of his suspects, someone to be interrogated, bullied and pushed around.

"Oh?" His tone was smooth, inviting; much smoother than the look in his eyes. That voice was another thing the FBI probably issued its agents on their first day on the job, to go with the suits. And the guns, although she hadn't seen Patrick's yet. She didn't doubt he carried one. There was something about him. That intensity, it had a purpose beyond getting answers. Or undressing women visually. She had seen it before; he was a man with a long-term goal, and Lord help the person who got in the way.

All right, maybe that was unfair. But she could practically smell the ambition in him, and it made her wary. Lily didn't understand ambition. She had needs, desires, of course. Everyone did. But ambitious people carried a tension around inside them that made her tense up in return. She preferred the company of those who were comfortable where they were, who took days one at a time and who didn't ask too much of life.

"There's an old joke," she said, shaking off her reaction and responding to his earlier question. "'Dogs have owners, cats have staff.' Or, 'Dogs come when called. Cats have answering machines and might get back to you.' All true. A cat will do something you ask of it because it chooses to do so. It won't obey out of loyalty, or fear, or even love—merely choice."

Cats couldn't be used. Not that way. It was one of the reasons why she respected them.

Agent Patrick nodded, not laughing, or even smiling at her words. "And cats choose to listen to you?"

No. Cats chose to talk to her. They always had, even when she was a little girl and terrified of them. They would come to her, twine their lithe bodies around her ankles, look up at her as though she could solve great mysteries, and she would curl into a ball against the nearest wall and cry until her mother came and got her. She never got violent, the way some phobics did, and she never got angry—just sad to the point of over-whelming depression. She had *wanted* to like cats, in a way she never felt with people.

"My boss at the shelter claims I must smell like catnip, or something."

The look in his eyes suddenly shifted. Lily wasn't sure how, or why, but the interest deepened, his face changing slightly. It made her suddenly uneasy in a way even his previous intensity hadn't, as though she had suddenly been dumped somewhere unfamiliar, without warning. The other man, the FBI agent, she knew how to avoid, and why. This man, the one with the glitter-bright stare, he was... *Seductive* was the only word that came to mind. Seductive, and danger-ous, and appealing. Which were three words, but all meant the same thing. He was looking at her as if he wouldn't mind taking a roll in some catnip, himself, right then. Like he wasn't undressing her now, but was already inside her.

Lily knew herself pretty well. She was attractive, if you liked brunettes, too short, and had a reasonably curvy, if not stacked, body. Great hair, nice face. A

solid B-grade on all fronts. Nice, but nothing that quali-
fied for that kind of fascination. He was interrogating
her again, only with a different question in mind.

"Look, I don't know what Detective Petrosian
thought I'd be able to tell him, or what you think I can
do. I'm good with cats, yes. But—"

"Have dinner with me."

"Excuse me?" She should have been expecting that,
yet it still caught her off guard.

His thin lips curved in a smile now. The hint of white
teeth showed between the pale red flesh, but the intensity of his eyes was, if anything, even more focused on
her. Not undressing her, but getting inside her brain.
Inside her soul.

She recoiled, and then scolded herself for recoiling.

All right, Lily, stop that, she told herself. *You're tired,
stressed and overreacting. He's just a guy. A cute guy.
Why not have dinner with him?*

"I'm a federal agent, miss. You can trust me." She
must have laughed at that. "Seriously," he went on. "I
have a few questions I want to ask you, but I just hit
town and I'm starving. And we hijacked you out of your
job—the least I can offer is dinner, as a thank-you for
your help."

Lily was oddly flattered, but shook her head. She
wasn't much for dating, and even if she were, a guy who
was in town for two, three days tops? She needed more
time than that to make up her mind about a guy. Even
if he was as exotic as a Burmese, and friendly as a
Maine coon. And on the hunt sure as any big cat she'd
ever seen. "Thank you, but no. I'm just going to grab a

ride back to the shelter, pick up my car and go home. It's been a really long day and I'm not feeling particularly social. Detective Petrosian has my phone number and e-mail address, if you need to ask me anything more, but I'm sure there's nothing I can add."

She stood up, and then looked down at the agent, remembering that moment of sympathy she had experienced on the scene, over the bodies of the kittens. "Whoever did this, you'll find him."

It wasn't a question, and Agent Patrick didn't pretend otherwise.

"Yes, ma'am."

Petrosian found him half an hour later still sitting at the table, a notepad flat in front of him, the unlined paper covered with circles with words scribbled inside them.

"So what's the story?" he asked the cop, pushing the notepad away from him in disgust.

"The store was for rent. Last owner moved out four months ago, but market's been slow, hasn't even had anyone in to look at the space since then. It was the Realtor who found the bodies, called us in."

"Four months." Patrick reached for the pad and jotted that down as well. "We'll need a list of anyone who might have known about the space, had access to the keys, that sort of thing."

"Already have someone on it. Anything else you want us to dig into?"

Jon T. Patrick was smart. More, he was savvy. And he knew blue sarcasm when he heard it. So he dragged himself out of his thoughts and gave the detective his full attention. "You guys have it under control. I'm just working a side investigation, is all. A little project."

"Uh-huh." Petrosian maybe wasn't as smart, but he was plenty savvy too, so he let Patrick's comment go without challenge.

"Although…" Patrick knew it was stupid, but he couldn't resist. "Tell me about your specialist, Ms. Malkin."

Ms. Malkin. Lily. It wasn't a name that suited her: a lily was a delicate, overscented flower. Malkin's hazel eyes were tough, her body toned and muscled under the curves, her stride strong, and her scent…unscented. Powder and soap.

He usually liked perfume on a woman, liked placing his face against her neck and smelling the aroma rising off her skin. But perfume would be wrong on Malkin. It would be overkill.

He wanted to take her out to dinner. Nothing fancy: pasta maybe, and a bottle of decent wine. He wondered if she drank red wine. He thought maybe she did. Or maybe he was projecting. Patrick was amused at himself, despite the seriousness of the case. Profiler, profile thyself? Why was he so attracted to her? She was a hot little thing, yeah, but he'd seen better. But there was something about her that spoke to him, beyond the physical, and well beyond any use she might have to the case.

That attraction was bad. He couldn't afford to be distracted. He had a steady rule: no female distractions on a case. After, yes. But he would be on his way home by then.

Petrosian looked at him carefully, and then answered. "Lily's good people. She works as a teller down at West Central, that's a local bank. Volunteers at the shelter. Lived here, oh, three, four years? About that. Went to school on the West Coast, doesn't seem to have any family that she's mentioned. Straight up, all straight up."

"And she talks to cats." She also had skin the color of a sun-ripened peach. He wondered if all of her skin was that exact tone.

Petrosian snorted. "She does something, that's for sure. Years ago, I was a rookie, we had a cougar wander into town, get panicked. The local zoo sent over one of their people to try to get it back into a cage. Took us all night, half a dozen tranqs, and earned me a couple of nasty gashes before we got the damn thing cornered and caged. Last year? Lily damn near purred a big cat into walking on its own paws into the cage. Took maybe an hour, all told."

Patrick wasn't sure he entirely believed that, but they'd probably both seen stranger things in their years. "How does she do it?"

The cop shrugged. "Don't know, don't care, and she won't thank you for poking around."

Patrick sat back in his chair. It wasn't a warning-off. Quite. But he wasn't on the prowl; he wasn't going to do anything that would hurt her. His interest in her was about the case; he really *did* have questions he wanted to ask her. A traditional expert would be by the book. This case didn't feel by the book. The cats had been clean and well cared for, and killed with what could almost have been reverence. Maybe talking to the cat talker would give him the point of view he needed to understand how and why.

Petrosian looked at the schoolhouse-style clock on the wall. "I'm still on shift. I've got other cases to deal with before they let me out of here. A patrolman will take you to your hotel. If we catch any new info, I'll give you a call."

That was a clear dismissal. Slaughtered animals were a crime, but they weren't a high-priority one, not even in a relatively sleepy New England city. FBI man could do whatever he wanted, but the cops weren't going to hold his hand while he did it. That suited him fine, actually.

Still, Petrosian lingered. "You going to need anything else for your 'little project' before I sign off on the paperwork?"

"No, I think I have everything I need for now." Clearly, he was supposed to skedaddle, as his mother used to say. Patrick closed his notebook and stood, feeling the joints in his knees and hips creak distressingly. He wasn't getting old, just road-worn. He'd been on another assignment when the call came about this find. He'd barely had time to hand over his notes to another agent and throw some clean clothing into a case before catching his flight to Newfield. "I think I'll grab some dinner and do some more research."

"You do that."

Petrosian watched him walk out; Patrick could feel the man's gaze between his shoulder blades, like an infrared targeting mechanism. But he had been in cities where the cops were actively hostile, not just cautious, and he had learned not to take offense where none was intended.

The hotel he'd been booked into was pretty standard: a decent enough bed, small bathroom, inexpensive toiletries. But it had hot water, a desk he could work at and a twenty-four-hour restaurant next door. All the comforts of home. But somehow, showered and dressed, his notes spread out in front of him and covered with his scribbles and yellow Post-its, he wasn't in the mood to work, or to go downstairs and eat alone.

You're on the job, he told himself. *Don't be an idiot. The lady said no, and you shouldn't have asked in the first place anyway.*

Not letting himself think about it, he pulled out his cell phone and dialed the phone number he had jotted on the edge of his notebook before handing back the original file to the police clerk.

"Lily Malkin? It's J.T. Patrick. Agent Pa—yes, that's right. Hi. Look, I know you said that you weren't interested in dinner, but I really want to bounce some ideas off you, and…well, I hate eating alone. Especially when I'm away from home. In a new town. Save me?"

Chapter 3

Lily stared at the phone, not quite believing what she had just heard. Did he know how obvious that line of bullshit was? He had to; she could practically hear it in his voice: "Laugh at me, but laugh *with* me."

"Agent Patrick…"

She shouldn't. She really shouldn't. He was far too appealing, and her thoughts had been far too depressing. Against her better judgment, she said yes.

"Great. Nothing fancy—maybe there's a local Italian around here, a mom-and-pop place you could recommend? I'm craving ziti."

She knew exactly the place, and on a Tuesday night, it shouldn't be too crowded. "I'll pick you up in—" she looked at the clock on her desk "—twenty minutes?"

"Great. I'm at the Veis Hotel, over on—"

"I know where it is. Budget central—nice to know our tax dollars aren't going to Jacuzzis and wet bars."

He snorted into the phone. "Hardly. I'll see you in twenty."

She hung up the phone and stared down at the pile of bills she had been paying. Or trying to pay, as her thoughts had been more on this afternoon's scene than what she owed Visa and the electric company. "You. Are insane. And this is a terrible idea."

Ten minutes later she had gone through three different outfits, finally settling on a pair of black slacks and a dark red sweater, with her favorite boots with the heels that made her feel not quite so short. Jeans were fine for shelter work, but even a casual dinner with a good-looking guy seemed to call for something a little more. Or at least something not covered in cat hair.

She stared in the mirror, giving herself a once-over. A rub of blush over her cheekbones, and eyeliner and that was it. The look was casual, not too much effort, but looking good. Grabbing her keys off the hook by the door, she was in her car and on her way before she could second-guess herself.

Lily Malkin wasn't much for impulsive actions. She felt more comfortable on her own, when she could control the situation, and not have to do anything other than what she wanted. Her father called her selfish, but among all the men she had dated—and the few she had loved—Lily had never met anyone that she honestly felt that she could relax with; that she felt could accept her for who she was.

Probably because she was never quite sure who that was. An insomniac, not-quite-cat-phobic, detail-oriented female with trust and responsibility issues, to start. In short, a mess. On her own, Lily could deal with it. Bring someone else into the equation, and there were too many variables. Too many ways things could go wrong. So control was important.

After graduating from college, she had gone into banking because she wanted a job that would allow her to interact with people, but from a safe distance, and would allow her to leave the job at the office. Being a bank teller was perfect. She had moved to Newfield after a lot of thought, choosing it for low cost-of-living and a pretty environment.

Even working at the shelter had been part of a long-term planned goal. Tired of having responses to stimuli she could not control, she had finally gone to a therapist who helped her gain the courage to stop avoiding cats, and face the discomfort. It had worked, but the process had been slow, steady, and under her control every step of the way.

She was having dinner with this man because…

Lily knew the reason. Because she couldn't get the image of those kittens out of her mind, and he was the only way to get answers about who would do that sort of thing. And why.

If she could help him find this guy, then maybe this feeling of depression, of helplessness and failure, might go away.

It had nothing to do with the way his eyes were so dark, or intense. Really. It was all part of the long-term plan.

"And if he suggests dinner in his hotel room, you are out of there, federal agent or not," she told her reflection in the rearview mirror. Her reflection looked dubious, and she laughed at herself. Right now, she was so tired she'd probably fall asleep in the middle of anything, anyway.

To her relief, he was waiting outside the hotel's lobby when she pulled up, talking on his cell phone. He saw her and waved, then closed the phone and slipped it into his pocket. He had a slim leather briefcase with him, she noted, and when he slipped into her Toyota she noted there were a number of color-coded files sticking out of it. This really was going to be a working dinner, then. Lily almost laughed again at the wash of disappointment she felt.

They were seated quickly; as expected, the little Italian restaurant wasn't busy, and they had the corner to themselves. Patrick put the file on the table next to him and quickly buttered a bread stick. "Sorry. I'm a carb addict, if there's one thing I can't resist it's fresh bread."

"It is so unfair. Guys can eat anything and not gain a pound." Casual, almost stupid chitchat. They were doing it to keep from thinking about what they had seen that afternoon. Or at least, she was. If she could not think about it, she could keep it from being so real. If it wasn't real, maybe it wouldn't hurt so much.

I'm sorry, kittens, she thought again, feeling the wave of helplessness move through her. There was nothing she could have done, and yet she felt overwhelmed by the feeling that she was *supposed* to have done something, somehow prevented this.

He protested the implied slur in her words. "Pound,

shmounds. This particular guy has to keep up with the FBI regs for fitness. They don't let us relax until after we have seniority behind a desk. That's why we're all so anxious to get promoted."

She laughed, almost more than what the joke was worth. He glanced at her quickly, looked at the menu, then looked at her again, those dark eyes toned down for once. "Lily. Before we talk about anything else… I'm not a practicing psychologist, but it's okay to be upset. What you saw…most people never run into that kind of violence, and that's good. Nobody ever should, whether it's directed at them or someone or something else. And when you do see it, you shouldn't be unaffected. It's not healthy, or human, to be unaffected. Even us tough federal-lawman types."

She toyed with the corner of the menu, rubbing it between two fingers. "I know. It's just…how do you sleep? After things like that?"

He gave the faintest shrug, barely a jerk of his shoulder. "I catch the people responsible. Or I do my damnedest to try, anyway. That is why I need to pick your brains. I think you can help me."

She pursed her lips, weighing his words. "All right."

Something she hadn't even known was knotted inside her eased with those words. She only meant to agree to having her brain picked in exchange for dinner, but somehow it felt as though it was more.

Is this it? she wondered. Is this the thing I've been feeling I need to do? That easy? She doubted it. But it was something.

They placed their orders, and Lily ordered a glass of

wine—"None for me," Patrick said regretfully. "I'm technically on duty. On the plus side, that means I can expense this, so eat up!"

There was something about him, despite his practiced charm, despite his intensity, that almost made Lily forget her original discomfort. Almost. He cared about what he was doing. That made him likable. The fact that he was likable made her even more cautious. Charming men were men with agendas and ambition. Men with agendas and ambition were not to be trusted. It wasn't any one bad experience that had drummed that into her, although it was proved, more often than not. No, that knowledge, that wariness, was born in her, it sometimes seemed.

This wasn't a date, she reminded herself, wondering at his pleased smile at her choices. It was, as he said, a business meeting. Over food. So what if he had an agenda?

Everyone wanted something. Everyone had a secret. Even her.

"So why is the FBI investigating this?" she asked again, taking a bread stick for herself.

This time, unlike earlier that day, he answered her.

"The FBI normally gets called in for certain things. Kidnappings, bank robberies, crimes that cross state lines or involve national issues…. This…isn't really one of them." He cracked a crooked smile. "Except it falls in that gray area of 'might be of interest.' Courtesy of the twenty-first century and modern paranoia, just about every investigated crime gets entered into a national database. Mostly they just sit there, unless there's something in them that triggers an alert some-where else. In my case, I look for tags that indicate animal-abuse cases."

He waved the remains of his bread stick at her, as though lecturing. It should have been annoying, but wasn't, mainly because his intensity was so real, and focused on a *thing,* not her. Whatever it was that he did, it meant a great deal to him. She admired that.

"Animal abuse is—it's one of the things we're taught to look for in the background of suspects. I'm working on a particular theory that, if I can prove it, could lead us to a way to identify and stop potential killers. So, if a police department reports a notable case of animal abuse it pings on my radar. If there are certain elements to the case, I follow up."

"Certain elements?" The waiter came with her glass of wine and his soda. Lily nodded her thanks, but kept her attention on Patrick.

"A level of ferocity, or indications of repetition. Something that suggests escalation."

"That whoever it is, is getting ready to move on to something bigger," she guessed. "Like humans."

"Exactly. Abuse, especially of cats, is considered one of the 'terrible triad,' of indicators that's often found in the background of a serial killer. That, and arson, are historically two of the major warning signs of serial killers before they turn to human targets. It's almost as though they're trying to vent themselves on weaker beings, or—by some theories—are working up their nerve to go to the next level. Nobody really knows for certain. It's an inexact science."

Lily was horrified, but fascinated. Everyone knew about serial killers, of course—even if you never watched the nightly news, you had to have heard of *Silence of the Lambs*. But she had never realized that there was a pattern, or a science, to it. Or that cats were so very much a target.

"And you try to find them before then. But how do you know that they're going to go to people next?"

"I don't. Most of the time they don't, either. But if I can stop them before that line is crossed, that's all that matters. Law enforcement isn't all about punishment. It's about being a deterrent, too."

She nodded. It made sense. "So this one incident brought you out here?"

He hesitated, taking a sip of his soda before responding. "No. Not the one. This goes no further than this table, Lily." He paused until she nodded her agreement. "Three years ago in the next town, there was a couple of scattered cases—cats being cut open and left, like some kind of sacrifice. By itself, that's nothing, unfortunately. Wannabe Satanists, or just one kid with a cruel streak, or even a budding coroner who wanted to start small. They wouldn't even have been entered in the system, except there was a small media fuss.

"And that was nothing, until now. The reason they called me is that here have been two incidents prior to this in the past two months. All involving cats. All young males. None of them quite so…formalized as today's offering. Whoever this guy is, assuming it's the same guy from three years ago—he's working out a pattern that satisfied him. If it was him three years ago…

he's on an evolving scale, an escalating one. And that's a major danger sign."

"So you think…" She shuddered involuntarily. "You think we have a baby serial killer right here in Newfield?"

She'd had nightmares about that; not often, maybe three or four times, but unlike most of her dreams they tended to stay with her even after she woke: of women dying, one after another, in terribly bloody ways. She hated those dreams, all the more so for never being able to figure out what caused them or how to prevent them.

"No." He shook his head, almost as though he regretted that lack of serial killerage. "The indicators I've seen so far suggest that he hasn't crossed that line. I'm not sure that's the direction he's going in, either. His pattern is… Different. Odd. Intriguing."

Lily cocked her head and studied him. "You find strange things intriguing, Agent Patrick."

He accepted the jab with self-aware good humor. "Nature of the job, Ms. Malkin."

The conversation was interrupted by the delivery of their meals, and the resulting pause to sort things out.

"No," he said again once they started eating. "I don't think he's a serial killer. The specifics line up—cats, violence, repetition. That's what pinged on my radar. But seeing it—the feel of it is all wrong."

"Intriguing?"

"To a person with my background, yes. Serial killers have a variety of reasons for acting the way they do, by their standards. The files—" and he made a gesture with his fork to the file at his side "—the first two cases, and now this one, they don't show the kind of…passion normal to a serial killer's buildup. This was…"

"Restrained."

He looked at her with surprised respect. "Yeah."

Lily didn't know why she had said that, but when she thought about it, it was true. The violence had been contained, the cats carefully tended, the scene almost designed, like a stage set….

Going back there made her insides queasy again, so she changed the subject. "So what's the third thing? You said there was a—terrible triad? You said two, so what's the third?"

"Bed-wetting."

Lily stared at him. "Bed-wetting."

"It shows up often enough in established serial killers that it's considered an indicator, yes."

She wasn't going to laugh. It wasn't funny. "But not a crime."

"No, not a crime. We don't investigate anyone on the basis of soiled linens."

"I'm not laughing," she told him.

"Nobody ever does," he assured her, his dark eyes creased around the edges with humor. "Joking is frowned on in the FBI."

Lily ate a few bites of her veal, letting the moment pass intentionally, and then looked up at her companion. "All right. You said you wanted to ask me something about the case. About the cats?"

He took a bite of his own ziti, chewed and swallowed before responding. Good table manners, she noted.

Another point in his favor, were she keeping any sort of list. Which she wasn't.

"Yeah. About the cattery that you said he had. You work in a shelter—it looks like you have a full house there?"

"Always. Females, unless they're fixed, breed regularly even when they have kittens already. Even if you could stop every stray from breeding tomorrow, there would be more cats in shelters than we could ever find homes for."

Lily felt guilt once again for not adopting one or two of her own. She had the room, and Lord knew she had gotten over her fear…but something held her back from bringing them into her own home. She still needed that distance, the place to retreat to, in case things went wrong.

"So why was he breeding them, if there are so many out there to adopt?"

"For color." No hesitation in her mind now, not after what Patrick had told her. "He—we're assuming a he?"

"For now."

"All right. He used spotted tabbies with white paws, all seven of them. The cats before, they were spotted as well?"

Patrick nodded. "According to the files the cops gave me, yes. Not all of them had the white paws, though. That was new."

"The spotted markings are common enough, but not so much so that you could find seven of them, all about the same age—not kittens, but less than two years old, I'd guess. And to find three…three batches of seven?

The combination of color and age, there's no way he could assume he was going to find them all at the same time. So it makes sense he'd try to breed them himself."

"That was my thought, too. This guy, whoever he is, wasn't flying off the cuff. He has an agenda. There was planning here, at least a year's worth to be breeding his own litters. More, since the first incident was two months ago, and the cats were about the same age."

"But why?" Why would someone do something like this? Why use cats? Why cats of that specific type? "And God, how could he breed cats, raise them and then *kill* them?"

Patrick poked his fork at the mound of ziti on his plate, and then looked up at her, his dark eyes now shadowed by more than exhaustion. "I don't know. But I'm going to find out."

Then he leaned back and smiled at her, clearly changing mental tracks. "But enough. You've confirmed what I suspected, and may yet be useful to the investigation, so this meal is hereby considered a justified expense. Therefore I'm not going to do anything right now except enjoy the lovely company, the excellent food and the fact that I'm not cooped up in a hotel room watching reruns of Fox shows I didn't like when I first saw them. And I insist that you do the same, just to keep me company."

Lily flushed, but smiled at him, and went back to her veal piccata, hyperaware of the fact that he was watching her every move, observing her the same way he had observed the crime scene. Charming, but ambitious, she reminded herself. Be careful.

"So. You volunteer with cats and work in a bank. And, occasionally, help out the local cops and wandering feds. What else does Ms. Lily Malkin do?"

Lily didn't play games, was what she didn't do. "I bake. I work out to burn off the calories I put on from baking. I sleep as much as humanly possible. I like modern art and Delta blues, an occasional glass of wine and really scary movies with buttered popcorn. I have no siblings, my father lives in Seattle where I grew up and my last relationship ended amicably. Anything else?"

He blinked, visibly thinking over her words. "No, I think that about covers everything, and then some. Your turn."

She didn't have to think about that at all. "What does the T stand for?"

"The letter T," he said easily, and she smiled reluctantly in return. Oh, charming. Very, very charming. But she still wasn't going to play.

Lily turned off the beeping alarm even before she turned on the light as she came in through the garage. Once the condo was plunged back into silence, she slipped her shoes off at the door, dropped her bag on the dining-room table and shuffled to the narrow spiral staircase that led to the bedroom. She had lived in a studio apartment when she first came to town, but on her morning run one day she had passed the row of town houses under construction and, on a whim, stopped in at the builder's office. Three months and most of her savings later, she had closed on her town house, and two months after that she had moved in.

It was the first place she had ever owned, the first real home she'd had since leaving her father's home for college sixteen years before. Her dad had choked up when she called to tell him the news. Her dad was a little weird: "not married? No problem, honey, you'll find someone some day. But this endless string of living in apartments? That can't be healthy!"

The condo wasn't large—a kitchen, living room and dining room downstairs, and a bedroom and bathroom upstairs—but it was all hers. Her refuge.

She stripped as she went into the bathroom, tossing her clothing into the hamper and turning on the shower. The two glasses of wine at dinner, plus a hot shower, might be enough to let her get to sleep—and *stay* asleep until the alarm went off. If she was lucky, and fate was kind, she might not even dream.

Or if she did, maybe they would be the hot and sexy kind. Lord knows, she had enough material to work with tonight.

"Don't get so caught up in secret-agent-man fantasies that you forget to finish paying those bills," she told herself, pulling her hair into a scrunchie and knotting it. She was on shift at the bank from ten to four, and if she didn't get everything into the mail in the morning, it would bother her all day.

The mirror was starting to fog, and she rubbed a spot clear to check her skin.

"Holy shit!" she shrieked, spinning around.

There was nothing there, of course. She had known there wasn't going to be anything there. It wasn't possible that there was anything there—the alarm had been on, no windows had been open. There was no way a cat could have gotten in.

There was no way she could have seen, reflected in that tiny corner of the mirror, a cat sitting on the shower ledge behind her, watching her with wide, rounded green eyes.

Mrrrrrai?

And there was no way she could hear the plaintive query of a cat, echoing off the tile of the shower, over the sound of the water and the rasp of her own breath.

Lily took a deep breath; slow in through her mouth, out through her nose. "I'm tired. I've had a stressful day. I probably should not have had rich food and red wine on top of that. I'm hallucinating."

Mrrrrraaw.

"And I don't need you laughing at me, either," she told the phantom cat, getting into the shower and, against her original intentions, pulling the scrunchie out and putting her head entirely under the falling water, letting the steam and sound drive everything else away.

"Just let me sleep tonight," she said: a prayer to whoever might be listening. "No dreams. No staring at the ceiling. Just…sleep."

Somehow, she didn't think that was going to happen.

Chapter 4

He didn't like it here. The basement wasn't a good place. It was too damp, and too cold, and the off-white concrete floor absorbed the smells no matter how much bleach was dumped on it. But he had run out of other options; after his last failure, the authorities were watching empty spaces too closely, and he dared not openly rent anywhere, not with all the beasts he would have to bring with him.

This would have to do.

He finished scrubbing the table, and paused to wipe sweat off his face. He smelled as bad as the bleach and piss combined. There was no way She would come to him smelling like this. He needed to be clean, oiled and scented, and appropriately dressed, or even the very best sacrifice would be in vain.

The creatures around him were listless, most with their bellies distended with pregnancy. God, they were disgusting. Too long to wait, and nowhere to find new ones. Only four males were right, and he needed seven, but he couldn't wait any longer.

The appeal had failed again. He was close, so close, and yet the key would not turn; She would not come. Three years he had waited, since waking: three years counting cycles and watching the signs. Only once each turning was it right, and the doorway was only open so long; if he didn't find the right combination, it would close and lock and he would be forever on the wrong side, all he hoped to gain gone for yet another year.

Seven times three was a lucky turn; this would be the time. Three times to be lucky.

Seven was the number, was a holy number, all his instincts told him so, the same way he knew he would know Her when she came. There were no books, no guides to show him the way: instinct was all he had to go on. Instinct had told him who he was, what he must do. Instinct was all he could trust.

He glanced up into the sky. The moon. The moon was key. The dark moon was coming, and all the steps had to be taken before then—when She waxed full again, it would be too late to try again until the cycle passed again. But the faster he worked, the less perfect the beasts. He needed to find some way around that, something to make the offerings acceptable. And soon, soon! When the final offering was made, it had to be perfect!

A cat *mrrrowed*, low and angry, and another answered, setting an entire cage of the things off.

"Shut up!"

It wasn't fair! He didn't understand the urgency that drove him, or the knowledge that filled him, but they were the only things that had any reality, any substance. Everything was *wrong* suddenly, since that moment three years ago when his old existence had disappeared and left him in this hell. There was nothing inside him now except for that urgency. His brain could focus only on the things he needed, the steps he must take. All sensation, all joy, was gone: he woke in the morning and the sky was the wrong shade of gray, the air the wrong smell, the speech of those around him the wrong sound.

Only when he drifted back into the dream was everything made right again. Only then did he feel whole. The dream of what was through the doorway, his rightful, long-denied prize. Her, and the knowledge She would bring.

Everything he did, the steps he went through, they were all toward that.

"Water, water, everywhere, all for the beasties to drink," he chanted. He poured water from the jug into plastic dishes, placing each one in a cage, careful to move so as not to actually come into contact with any of the creatures. The gleam in the beasts' eyes taunted him, made him dizzy. They judged, they always judged, the damn things, as though they were somehow better than he was.

Damn things. How he hated them. Hated them! They were cruel, and faithless, and they betrayed....

"Calm, calm," he crooned, his voice a deep, soothing baritone that made the cats' ears flicker to attention as he passed, his left hand reaching up to touch the palm-size amulet hanging under his sweatshirt. "Follow your courses and be thorough. They're only animals. They don't know a thing."

But they did. They were the keepers of the secret wisdom, the knowing of old. The ancient secrets he needed. Their blood would bring Her, and She would bring the way home.

Fantasy and myth, but there was truth at the bottom of it, he knew. "They don't know, but you do, yes, you do. You remembered, you did."

Three years before. Something came to him in the night, a sudden click in the brain that set him on this path. The first time he had faltered. But now, now all he needed was to find the right key, the right combination and he would be free of this wrong existence. No longer powerless and drab but allowed to claim what was his, what had always been meant to be his.

Whatever that was.

The doubt touched his mind briefly, and he shook it off. It had been within grasp once, before She failed him, denied him. Ruined it all. Not this time. The beasts were the way. The beasts knew the answer. The thought soothed him, calmed him enough that he could continue.

He finished his chores and made sure all the cages were locked, then closed the basement's door behind him, letting the silence enrobe him. Silence was so much better. He hated the sound the beasts made; it caused his skin to crawl. He would have torn their tongues out if something hadn't warned him against it.

Use them, yes. They were part of the key. But do not harm them. Never harm them. That would undo it all.

He climbed the stairs, the solid tap of his boots against the concrete forcing him to focus, to put the basement into a compartment and close the door, to replace the mask that he wore, so others would not know him until it was time.

A passing memory—red slipped against black cloth, harsh panting and white claws—confused him for a moment, but he shook it off. The past was failure. The future was still to come. The future was in his control.

He opened the door, and felt dawn's cool air on his face. It was moist with rain-to-come, and he lifted his face to better enjoy it.

"Hey. You!"

A guy with an apron, a broom in hand, staring at him. Why? His mask. He needed to replace his mask, pretend to be one of *them* again. But the panic hit him, and he couldn't remember how.

"You sick or something? Get out of there!"

The exit from the basement led to an alley next to the man's store. The ground was disgusting, filthy. Cold. The damp suddenly seeped into his bones, and he shivered. He was always cold.

Not daring to say anything to the man, he brushed past him, hunched into his jacket, walking away. His mask came back to him too late, and he lifted his face to stare back at the man, willing him to remember this face, not the other.

Someday soon he would find his way home. Then he

could show his true face, his gods-given face, and they would know what he was, and the power he wielded. Then they would treat him with respect. With *fear*.

Chapter 5

Lily shoved her face into the pillow, her shoulders hunching up to her ears, as though trying to make herself into a small, unattractive target. The sheets tangled around her while she dreamed, creating an almost mummy-like wrapping around her. Darkness. Pain. Loss. A sense of failure as endless as the night sky curving over her. She wept, despair settling over her, seeping into her bones, her very being.

Then, out of the darkness, a faint sound. A hint. A suggestion. For the first time, a lifeline.

Mrrauu?

Her head lifted, deep in the dream. This was different. This was new. *Yes, yes. I hear you.*

Mrrauu! Like a beacon easing her out of despair,

bringing her away from the pitiless sky. *Mrrauu!* Commanding, imperious, the call demanded attention be paid, and paid now!

Her shoulders relaxed, her entire body softening, easing into the mattress as the dream took her over, bringing her out of nightmare into something more pleasant….

A shadow danced impatiently ahead of her, green eyes glinting in the lamplight. Her laughter spilled out over the doorsill, the sound bright as moonlight over the still-warm sand. "I am yours to command, my beautiful. Only allow me to dress myself first, before you drag me into the night."

Mrrauu! Now! The moon is dark and it is time to dance, silly two-legged one! But she laughed as well, a rumbling purr and a small pink tongue.

A moment of peace, a moment only, and then a shift as often happens in dreams: the moonlight turned cold, the voices harsh and cruel. Lily moaned in her sleep, pulling her legs up to her chest as though to protect herself. Familiar territory, this: an old familiar dream, but not a friend, no.

The warm sands underfoot became unyielding: cold, root-strewn and treacherous. Soft linen became coarse cotton, scraping against wind-chafed and broken skin. The weight of metal draped around her wrists and waist, and only the comfort of a small soft body was the same.

Then the cat's cry elongated, filled with fear and outrage as that comfort was pulled from her grasp, and hard hands grabbed and pulled, shoving her forward

*into darkness. The flare of fire in front of them brought
no comfort, but sparked a scream from feline and
human throat at the same time, as though they were
one and the same....*

Lily sat upright, her throat scraped raw as though she
had strep, her eyes streaming and her sinuses dry as
though all the moisture had been sucked out of her
body. The horrific images wrapped around her, making
her shake and shiver despite the warmth of the room.

"My lady! My lady, forgive me!"

The sounds that came from her mouth were gibberish, and yet Lily felt that they were actual words, if she
were only able to understand them. And with the
sounds, the memories faded, not disappearing, but re-
treating enough that she was able to remember who she
was, where she was. That it was not her flesh aflame,
not her neck snapped, not her skin flayed from her body
while she yet lived....

Lily shoved the sweat-soaked sheets off her body
and hugged her pillow to her, waiting while her heart-
beat slowed to a more normal pattern. The usual cool
comfort of her bedroom seemed unfamiliar, alien
somehow, and that was almost more disturbing than the
nightmare itself.

Lily had suffered from nightmares since puberty,
dreams that left her sweat covered and crying. Even on
nights when she did not dream, she slept fitfully, aware
that one could strike at any time. Sleeping aids only
made it worse, forcing her to sleep without the ability
to wake up when a nightmare came.

In self-defense, she had studied not only the science

of dreams but the subject of her own, as much as she could remember. Cats crying in fear, nighttime assaults, and flashes of rage and death. Over the years, she had come up with a theory: that she was dreaming about the witch trials, here in New England, and similar events in Scotland, England, France and Spain. Anywhere the fear of women and cats had grown into such murderous depths. She had read about them, at some point, maybe when she was in school. It was a reasonable theory, and all tied into her problem with cats somehow, or grew out of it, or something.

Knowing that should have made her able to get rid of the nightmares, or make them easier to deal with.

It didn't.

Lily let the sweat dry on her skin, and let the details slide ever further from her grasp. The truth was that she didn't want to remember. It was awful, whatever it was. But there had been something new in this dream, something…she didn't remember details, but there was a vague sense of it being…nice.

"Not fair," she told the ceiling. "I'd like to remember the good things, at least."

Her therapist had told her once that it was the sign of an organized mind, to be able to separate nighttime fancies from waking reality. If that was true, Lily wasn't sure how disorganized people managed it, dragging the memory of such things with them throughout the day.

Thankfully, she seemed to have been born with an organized mind. True to form, by the time she was in the shower, rinsing out her hair, the images had faded almost entirely, and when she walked into the bank, greeting the other tellers and setting up her cash drawer, the only thing left was exhaustion, carefully hidden under coffee and a decent breakfast.

Her job was routine but not unpleasant, and she enjoyed the small interactions with the bank's customers. The day passed normally: the branch was the only one downtown, so they got a lot of foot traffic, especially between eleven and two when most people came in during their lunch break.

A tall, angular, gray-haired woman with a face cut from granite came up to Lily's counter. "Hello, Mrs. J."

The quintessential little-old-lady librarian, Mrs. Jablonsky came in on the second and sixteenth of each month to deposit her paycheck. According to town gossip, she had been a volunteer when the library first opened its doors in 1928, and had never left the job. When she died, they said, she would still be behind the desk, sorting returns and shushing kids who giggled too loudly in the computer room.

Kids were terrified of her. Lily thought she was fabulous.

"Hello, my dear. I can't believe that you're still here."

It was their own private joke. Mrs. J. knew what they said about her, and had more than once scolded Lily about following in her path, staying too long doing one thing over and over again, especially once they made her head teller.

"Don't you dare talk Lily into leaving!" Leanna cried from the next window. Lea was new, still in training, and still nervous enough about making a mistake that she wanted Lily to double-check every transaction she made.

"That's not going to happen," Mark said from the third open window. "She actually secretly runs the bank, it's just nobody's told the branch manager yet."

Lily shook her head, and finished Mrs. J.'s transaction, wishing her a nice day and going on to the person next in line. Mark was right, partially: she wasn't going anywhere. There was comfort in knowing what she would be doing each shift, every shift, and a comfort too in the combination of chatter and distance that her teller's window gave her. But she did wonder, occasionally, if there wasn't anything else besides working and volunteering at the shelter and having the occasional date that never seemed to go anywhere.

When things slowed down, she made sure that everyone else was set, then closed out her drawer and went into the backroom. She had intended to work on the shift schedule for the next week, but the moment she sat down her mind went blank, and she couldn't focus on the schedule sheet in front of her.

It had been twenty-four days since Aggie came and got her, brought her to look at an empty room of cages, and the bodies of murdered cats. Two days since the kittens had been killed, and if that bastard had done it before, he would do it again. Agent Patrick thought so, too. Somewhere out there, someone was raising cats for the sole purpose of killing them. Young male spotted cats. Three different instances, seven cats each. Or were there? Seven each time? Lily frowned, her pencil tapping the schedule form. It was an important point, but she didn't know why. She hadn't asked Agent Patrick that, during their dinner. Once he had finished asking her his questions, the evening had veered away from the case, covering more casual topics, as though...

As though they had been on a date. Which it hadn't been. Because she wasn't interested in dating an FBI agent. Especially an FBI agent who was only in town for a short time. Right? Right, Lily?

Worrying about the fact that she had no interest in dating a guy who hadn't asked her out was a better place to be than fretting over a cat killer. But not by much. She made an incoherent growl of frustration, and squeezed her eyes closed, trying to banish both thoughts and settle her brain on what she was supposed to be doing.

A penny dropped in front of her, ringing on the polished wooden desk and rolling onto the paper she was supposed to be filling out.

"I'd offer more for them, but I can't imagine you've got anything really tempting going on in there, the exciting life you lead."

"Very funny." She handed the penny to Mark, who added it back to his cash box.

"Actually, you looked way too intense for someone just trying to figure out who has to take the Saturday-morning shift. Come on, spill."

Mark was twenty-two, hyper, and about as able to keep a secret as a Hollywood talk-show host when the cameras were rolling. Even if she had been looking for a confessor, he would not have been it.

"Not a chance," she told him sweetly.

He pouted. "Bah, you're no fun."

"I'm your supervisor. I'm not supposed to be fun. Go away."

He laughed, and obeyed. Lily watched him go into the break room, and then heard the sounds of the mini-fridge opening and shutting, then the clatter of Tupper-ware and the *ding* of the microwave turning on. The smell of spicy rice and meat drifted back to her, and her stomach rumbled; she had leftover veal piccata for her own lunch, but she hadn't been hungry until that moment.

Shaking her head at how fickle the body was, she turned her attention back to the schedule sheet. Mark wanted off on Friday. Carole was on vacation. She had promised to take the Saturday-morning shift at the shelter; they were having another adoption drive, and it could get a little crazy if they had a good turnout… Trying to make everyone happy was impossible, but there was always a way to make everyone feel as if they had been listened to, even if they didn't get exactly what they wanted. You just had to work a little at it.

With a little willpower and a lot of determined rein-pulling when her mind wandered, the rest of the shift went easily enough. Once the week's schedule was fi-nalized, Lea's cash-out supervised and everyone's numbers tallied out, it was time to go home. Suddenly, her exhaustion came back with a vengeance.

Lily said good-night to her coworkers and walked into the dusk to her car, humming a tune that had been playing over the radio in the backroom, when a cat ran across her path and went under the cars parked nearest to her.

A shudder ran down her spine, involuntarily. She

wasn't superstitious, and she wasn't afraid, but something about the sight of the cat, its tail held high, triggered an old reflex. And if it was a spotted tabby… The shudder was back, brought on this time by the thought of what a stray cat might face if the cat killer found him.

Better check, she thought. You really won't sleep tonight if you think you left a cat out here at risk.

"Hey there." She bent down to see if she could get a better look at the cat; see if it was a stray, or someone's pet gone for an evening walk. "Hey, sweetie, come on out here."

The cat mrrowed once, a narrow, plaintive sound, and a strange sense of disorientation hit Lily. The call was familiar, as familiar as her own breathing, and yet somehow the sound itself sounded…wrong.

Do cats have accents? she wondered, a little giddy. Is this little one a transplant from somewhere else?

As soon as she thought that, the familiar parking lot fading out, replaced by something not familiar at all, and yet clear in every single detail….

The ceiling was far overhead, the walls open to the sun and wind, both soft today, thanks be to Ra. This would be difficult enough, without having to battle the elements as well as her heart.

"Bast's daughter." The shadow moved, scattering attendants like petals in his wake. "What news do you bring us, Priestess?"

The voice was deep and commanding, accustomed to both obedience and answers. She made a graceful obeisance as she drew forward. Her priestess rank might give her leeway within the palace's walls, but

respect must always be given where due, and antago-
nizing this man would not serve her purpose.

"You must do this for me," her lover had said as they
lay together on linen sheets, watching dawn slip over
the hills before them. "This one thing, and we shall reap
the benefits forever. Together."

A ping alerted Lily to the fact that she needed to get
gas. She made note of it as she backed her little Toyota
out of her parking space, and then stopped the car,
suddenly confused.

Hadn't she just been looking for a stray? She was
certain she had bent to look for the cat…but no, she was
in her car, everything in its place, and there was no cat
yowling a protest, locked in the carrier she always had
in her trunk, in case she needed to bring someone to the
shelter. The carrier that was still in her trunk, untouched.

Lily looked at the clock display on her dashboard: 6:42.

It had been six-thirty when she left the bank. She had
lost twelve minutes.

"You need a vacation, Lily Malkin," she told herself.
"Or more fresh air, if you're going to start losing time
like that." She rested her head against the steering
wheel, hitting it once, lightly, and then put the car in
motion again. It was just exhaustion, probably, and the
fact that her brain was still, inevitably, worrying about
the scene she had been exposed to the day before. She
had seen the cat, and…

And what? What had happened to the cat?

She waited at a red light and tried to remember.
There was nothing, a total blank spot, and then…
"Come on, kitten. Come on. *I don't have any sardines*

with me this time, I'm sorry. But I'll get you some later.
You know that you can trust me…."

You can trust me.

Then the noise came. Not a noise, a sound. A cat's
meow, echoing from under the car she was crouched
next to. An ordinary meow, not frightened or scared or
particularly hungry. Almost like a welcome-home
meow, a familiar greeting. And a request. From a cat
she had never seen before.

But there the memory ended, leaving her with a
sense of frustration and concern and a growing need
to *do* something.

First the cat in the shower, and now this. Either she
was heading for a nervous breakdown, complete with
aural and visual hallucinations, or…

She couldn't think of an "or" that made any sense.

The light changed, and the car behind her honked impatiently. "All right, all right, I'm going," she told the
guy, resisting the urge to flip him off. "And I'll call Aggie
when I get home, if he hasn't left a message. Obviously,
I'm not going to be able to relax until that guy's caught."

You could call Agent Patrick, a treacherous thought
snuck into her brain, and Lily squelched it. It had been
a lovely dinner. And that was that. She wasn't going to
give in to a foolish schoolgirl crush. Or even a foolish
adult crush. She would call Aggie; he would tell her if
anything new had come up.

The phone rang just as she opened the door from her
garage into the town house condo, and Lily felt her
heart race, just a little bit, with anticipation. She placed

the mail on the small table in the foyer and went to answer it.

"Yes?"

An obscure sense of disappointment flooded her when the caller turned out to be a telemarketer, rather than Detective Petrosian.

Or Agent Patrick, that treacherous voice said, practically pouting.

"Stop it," she told herself sternly, hanging up on the telemarketer midspiel. Yes, dinner had been enjoyable, despite the rather gruesome topic of discussion. But he was here on an investigation, and then he would be gone again. And she wasn't going to think about getting involved in a long-distance relationship after one dinner—and a working dinner at that!

"Especially since there is absolutely no reason to think that he's ever going to get in touch with you again," a different, more practical but equally annoying voice inside her head told her.

Lily laughed, and rubbed her face with both hands, smearing what was left of her eye makeup. "You're tired. And he freaked you out more than you realized with his talk about serial killers and whatnot." The fact that he didn't believe that the person who hurt those cats was, in fact, a serial killer, was reassuring…but she didn't like knowing that there was someone who thought it was okay, for whatever version of okay, to do that to innocent animals, either. And *why* had he done it? Not just once, but three times, if Agent Patrick was right, and all three incidents were linked?

Or maybe more than three times. The cops had found

three sites, but what Patrick had said suggested that
these guys didn't just start out full blown. They started
small, with one cat maybe. Then the thrill wore off, and
they had to—what was the word?—escalate.

Part of being the city's unofficial official cat specialist meant knowing when to actually *act* like one.

She wasn't an FBI agent or a cop. She couldn't do
anything to stop the guy. But there was something she
could do.

Picking up the phone again, Lily dialed a familiar
number.

"Felidae No-Kill Cat Shelter, Nancy speaking." Lily
could hear the sounds of a cat meowing in the background—they must have let Jones wander the halls
again. A twenty-pound panther-wannabe, Jones was
too big to be easily adopted, despite her sweet personality, so she had ended up being the office cat.

"Nancy, it's Lily. Is Ronnie in tonight? Can you get
her for me, please? Thanks."

When the director picked up the phone, Lily wasted
no time getting to the point. "Ronnie, I need you to okay
Halloween protocol, amended for any cat with a spotted
coat. Effective immediately, and especially for breeding
females and kittens."

The Halloween protocol was a ban on the adoption
of any black or mostly black cats the last few weeks of
October. Not every shelter did it, but the previous year's
incident—the one that had landed her an unwilling guest
spot on the news—had made them all deeply uneasy.
Ronnie's feeling had always been that anyone who
wanted a black cat on October 28 would still want it on

November 2, and she wasn't going to risk a cat on some crazy who wanted to sacrifice it to Satan or some other nonsense. The case just gave her the reason to enforce the ban.

"This has to do with your visitors yesterday?" Ronnie didn't know anything more than the fact that Aggie had come to ask her about something in an official capacity. There had been enough going on in the news last night to keep that relatively small story out of the limelight, and if it had been in the local paper, Lily hadn't seen it.

"Yes, and I can't say anything more, Ronnie, I'm sorry. But you might want to look and see if we adopted out any spotted tabbies, especially females, to anyone new in the past year. Especially someone new. Just in case the police need the information."

There was a slight hesitation, then Ronnie came through, making Lily let out a breath she hadn't realized that she was holding. "I'll have Mike go through the files tonight, if it's slow, Agent Patrick and I'll call the county shelter, too, let them know what we're doing. Is there anything we need to know that you can tell us?"

"Not really, no." Lily shrugged, even though the other woman couldn't see it. "I'm sorry. If I could, I would, really." Anything that affected the shelter was Ronnie's business, after all. But she didn't feel as if she could say anything more, at least not without checking with Aggie and Patrick first. "It's probably nothing. I'm probably just overreacting."

"Uh-huh." Ronnie's opinion of that came through loud and clear. They both knew that Lily—practical,

think-it-through, measure-twice-and-then-measure-again
Lily—didn't overreact.

Not unless there was cause.

"I'll see you tomorrow," Lily said, and hung up the
phone. It was after 7:00 p.m. and Aggie was off shift.
She'd make some dinner, and get some sleep, and talk
to him tomorrow morning.

Chapter 6

"You're our Fibbie?"

Patrick managed not to wince at the shelter receptionist's breezy greeting. "That would be me, yes." He wasn't exactly nostalgic for the bad old days when "Federal Bureau of Investigation" made people shiver, but sometimes familiarity really did breed contempt. Or worse. And how the hell did they know—he hadn't exactly been flashing his badge in the shelter....

The tiny redhead seemed inordinately pleased with herself. "We pulled the file together."

Patrick relaxed a little. Lily must have told them it was a federal priority, in order to get the material he had asked for so quickly. It wasn't a problem.

"There's not a lot of stuff. Adoptions slowed down

after the spring, and we actually had a run on reds and tiger stripes, not so many spotted." The redhead paused in her babble. "Which is weird, actually. Like Mother Nature knew this guy was coming and dried up the available pool. I mentioned it to a friend last night, and he said he hadn't seen any spotted or even many striped cats out and about either lately."

He accepted the inch-thick manila folder with a restrained sigh, tuning her chatter out. They'd managed to keep the killings out of the media, but there wasn't much you could do to stop gossip short of issuing a gag order, and the only way to ensure that would work was to actually gag the participants. Somehow, Patrick didn't think Lily would go for being gagged. Although…

Right. Brain on the job, Agent Patrick.

"Nancy, I'm going to bring the new calico into the soci—oh."

Speak of the devil.

"Lily."

She was wearing jeans again, topped with a red sweater, and high-top sneakers. Her mass of dark, curly hair was pulled back into a high ponytail that brushed her shoulders when her head turned. God, she was adorable.

"Agent Patrick." Something in his expression must have changed, because her face softened, and she relented. "Jon. Here for the files?"

He lifted his hand to show that he did, indeed, have the information. "Thanks for getting it together." The shelter had been more help so far than the local cops. And cops gossiped just as much, if not more.

"I just made a phone call," she said, dismissing his

thanks. "The staff here put everything together. I hope it's useful." She half turned, as though to go back into the shelter, away from him. Something about the slope of her shoulder reminded him of the curve of a cat's tail, the way it dipped and rose, and that triggered another thought in his head. Trying to nail it down, he held up a hand to stop her from leaving before it coalesced.

"Yeah?" she asked, pausing with a look he couldn't quite identify. Not suspicion, but…

"I'm going to ask another favor," he said, suddenly seeing a possible lead to follow, a thread to pull. His brain did that sometimes, seeing A and J and somehow coming up with 42. That was what made him good at his job; even when the lead didn't pan out, it brought them closer to something that might. Or a dead end, but you never knew until you investigated.

That's why the I was in FBI.

"Yes?" She was definitely wary now. He plowed on, the more he spoke the more solid the idea becoming in his mind. Somewhere in his brain he knew that he was imposing, asking too much of her, but he shoved it aside.

"I need you to do some digging for me. You said something that first night about a crazy who tried to adopt a cat last year for some kind of nasty use?"

"Yes…I had the shelter freeze all adoptions of cats matching the description of the ones this guy's been using, for the duration."

"Excellent, excellent. But you have had a problem in the past?"

"Yeah. Only once for us. But it happens all across

the country." She leaned against the wall, watching him. Nancy was looking from one of them to the other, like a spectator at a tennis match, clearly entertained.

He noticed her watching, and shook his head. "Is there somewhere we can talk?"

"We are talking, right here." Her chin was set on stubborn, he noted, and wondered what he had done this time. And why he knew that the way her jaw firmed like that meant she was feeling mulish.

"Lily." He meant it to be cajoling. It came out slightly amused, with a note of pleading. It seemed to work.

"All right. Come on." She led him into the back hallway, past a glass-walled room where dozens of kittens and cats frolicked on ropes and platforms. She pushed open a door and ushered him inside.

It was about the size of a broom closet, but with a soft carpet underfoot, and a bench covered in the same carpeting.

She noticed him looking around, clearly curious. "Meeting room. Where people can bond with a cat they plan to take home."

He was, reluctantly, impressed. "You guys have it all thought out, huh?" He had to admit that he had never really thought about what went into adopting out an animal.

"We try. Giving cats homes, it's maybe not up there with saving the world, but…"

"No, it's up there. All the studies say that people with pets are happier, healthier—better adjusted. If everyone had a cat to go home to, maybe I'd be able to stay home more often too."

Something happened there, right then: he felt it. A tangible connection between the two of them, the same thing he'd felt when they'd had dinner together. From the startled expression on her face, she had felt it—something—as well. He was suddenly aware of the fact that the room was very small, and they were standing awfully close together.

No. Oh, no. He did *not* have time for this.

"You had a favor you wanted to ask," she reminded him, trying to redirect the conversation.

"Yeah. Favor." A drop of sweat was forming on her upper lip, and he fought down the urge to lick it off. "I'm curious about the pattern of cat adoption, if there's a period of time that a certain type of cat's adopted, at a given time of year. And if any one type of person—male, female, old or young—adopts any one specific type."

"And you expect me to do all that, off our computers, in my spare time?" She started to laugh.

"What, you can't do it?" His smile was a challenge, but she was smart enough not to fall for it.

"Better men than you have tried to talk me into things, Agent Patrick. And no, that oh-so-charming smile of yours isn't going to work."

The smile, if anything, grew wider. "I'll take that under advisement. Do you think you'd be able to do a quick search, see what you can turn up—just for your own shelter, of course."

"Of course." Her dry sarcasm was almost off the chart, and he thought that he might just have to take her back to the hotel with him. Nothing sexual—okay, almost nothing sexual—she just managed to hit all his buttons, in a good way. A very good way.

Mind out of the gutter, Patrick. "Also, if you could see what turns up by way of rituals that might use circles rather than the traditional pentacle or whatnot? Specifically, anything that might signify or require the use of cats, or touch on cats in any way?"

Lily eyed him the way she might a particularly large, possibly rabid dog. "Oh, sure. Why not? You don't have some eager-beaver researcher at the bureau who handles this sort of thing with a mega supercomputer?"

He let go of the charm for just a second. "And by the time I got through channels just to request the paper-work, it would be next Tuesday already. This is so low down on the pole it's barely visible."

It wasn't fun to admit things like that—you always wanted to think that your case was the hottest thing on the wire—but the truth was, with nobody except a few stray cats threatened, it was a wonder they were letting him stay out here past the initial once-over ruled out an incipient serial killer. Taxpayers' dollars for his hotel room, et cetera. So long as he could make the case that this might lead to a better understanding of the deviant psychology that led to serial killers, his boss would give him rope, but the easiest way to do that was to make it as cheap as possible for the bureau. And that meant not calling on resources until he could justify them on more than a fishing trip.

If he was wrong, he wasted a little of Lily's time and the taxpayers' already allocated dollars. If he was right…he had a possible monograph to write on the topic, which would go into his personnel file, help build his theory and bring his name a little more recognition, and ease the next step upward on the ladder. Plus, possibly, someday it would help identify and capture a killer before he graduated to animals, much less humans.

It was all good.

He smiled at her again, bringing forward just enough charm to balance his need, and put on his best don't-make-me-beg face. She might say the smile didn't work, but he never let go of a proven tool. "Please?"

"I like you better when you aren't trying to be so damn charming," she told him, and walked out of the meeting room.

He blinked, and then grinned. A real grin, not the one he'd just been using.

"You, Jon T., just got nailed dead to rights."

He definitely wanted to wrap her up and take her home. And very much in a sexual way, too.

Several hours later, Lily still had a warm glow when she thought about the dumbstruck expression on Agent Patrick's face as she left him in the meeting room. It was almost—almost—worth spending her afternoon here, instead of going home the way she had planned.

She tucked one foot underneath her on the chair and closed a file, tossing it down onto the thick pile on the floor and opening another from the pile on the desk. Although going home would have been more useful. The shelter kept detailed records on what cats were adopted by whom, and when, including chipping details and medical history, but the color markings were often pretty vague, and even once they started attaching photos…well, she'd just say that the volunteer with the camera was no Diane Arbus.

"I can't believe I let him talk me into this," she said, tossing that file and dropping it to join the others. Several hundred down, another pile to go.

"Yes, it seemed as though it took so much arm-twisting and coaxing." Ronnie was sorting through piles at the desk across the office, her back to Lily. "Because you'd otherwise be off doing all sorts of exciting things…laundry was on the schedule for today, wasn't it?"

"There's nothing wrong with having a routine. It's very soothing to know what you're going to be doing, when. Plus, I need clean socks."

Ronnie just laughed. If Lily trusted Petrosian, she *liked* Ronnie. The older woman never tried to mother her, or be buddies, or anything other than her boss, with the clear structure of that relationship giving them both a place to stand. But there was no mistaking the fact that Ronnie *cared,* and cared enough to do it on Lily's terms.

"Lil?"

Nancy stuck her head into the office, her strawberry-colored mop of hair looking like a Day-Glo dandelion about to go to seed. "I was just about to shut down for the night—just wanted to let you know that your Fibbie's back."

Lily rolled her eyes heavenward. "Since when did he become *my* Fibbie? Don't anyone answer that. What does he want?"

"Dinner."

All three women jumped slightly when the agent appeared in the door next to Nancy.

"Sorry. I get sort of used to walking in, it's a badge thing."

Arrogance, Lily thought, practically oozed out of his pores. A sort of "you'll accept my right to do this" attitude that was all the more annoying because damned if Ronnie and Nancy didn't do exactly that.

She also hadn't realized that it was dinnertime already. The afternoon had slipped by without her noticing. They really needed an office with a window.

"Are you inviting, or demanding?"

The words were hanging in the air, pregnant with challenge, before she realized she was the one talking.

His dark eyes turned to her, and she shivered. How had she forgotten how intense his attention could be? No wonder Nancy jumped to fetch her. Far more effective than the charm, that.

"Demanding an invite?" he parried.

Ronnie laughed. "If you don't take him, I will, and Mike might be a little annoyed by that."

Lily blushed, and Patrick pressed his advantage. "Come on, you've spent all day doing research for me, dinner's the least I can do while you tell me what you found out."

Nancy, still in the doorway just behind the agent, nodded emphatically, making Lily blush even more. "Girl, you need to spend more time with the two-legged sorts, I told you that a dozen times."

Trying to recover from the three-pronged attack, she

picked up another file, then tossed it onto her desk and
gave in. "I agree…. Assuming your assumption was
correct that I've done research—of any duration—for
you at all."

He grinned again, supremely confident. She couldn't
resist. She didn't even try.

This time she took him to Toro Rojo. It was cheap,
cheesy and in no way could ever be considered a
romantic place to dine. He took her arm as they walked
from her car to the front door, and warmth spread from
the point of contact, all the way to and down her spine.
She would not shiver. She would not. She would—

"Are you cold?"

"No." She pulled open the door with a little more
force than was needed, and stepped ahead of him to give
her name to the waitstaff.

Behind her, she could hear him laugh.

"I don't suppose the police have made any break-
through discoveries about the identity of the—" She
stopped, not sure how you referred to the person they
were hunting. "Killer" seemed overblown; as much as
she valued feline life, it didn't seem right to put this
person on the same level as a murderer of humans. And
yet, anything else was too…soft.

"The unsub," he finished for her. "Which is profiler-
speak for nothing fancier than unknown subject of an
investigation, in case you were wondering. And no,
they have nothing. And I don't expect them to; Detective Petrosian was quite clear about the fact that they
don't have the manpower to follow up on a cruelty-to-

animals case when there's no owner in the picture to make a fuss."

He obviously expected her to protest that sort of dismissal, but she had been doing this long enough to understand the way things worked. Limited time. Limited manpower. You had to make choices in the world.

"So it's just us, then."

"Pretty much, yeah."

They were shown to their table and handed menus. Lily already knew what she wanted, so waited until Patrick had scanned the listings and made his decision before she continued.

"So are you going to be able to get any tax-paid support from the subpar and slow-moving resources of the federal government?"

He mimed a blow to the heart, the look in his dark eyes amused. "Why do I need them when I have you, oh most wondrous of cat talkers?"

"Keep that up and you'll be eating dinner in your hotel room. Alone."

That seemed to quiet him, at least for the moment, and she wondered at the kind of man who could find humor even in this discussion. Her own disorientation this evening was a clear sign that she, at least, couldn't be that glib. Then again, she had never been glib, not in her entire life.

"Seriously, I don't know what you hoped I might find. I'm not a researcher, I'm a bank teller. I deal with figures in, figures out, and everything balances up neat and tidy on a good day."

"And on a bad day?"

"It balances up neat and tidy, only it takes longer."

"Sounds like my job, actually," he parried, and she shook her head. Maybe it was the seriousness of his job, the seriousness of him, that needed that release in frivolity?

"Less bloodshed in my job."

He acknowledged the hit. "Good point."

Lily could feel herself starting to relax. This had been a good choice; never mind that she had groceries back home that were going to waste while she ate out. This was…different. She was helping with something important.

Yeah, sure, she told herself. And he's a lot easier to look at than television. Unless George Clooney's on, anyway.

"But I'm betting," he said, "that those vaunted tallying-up skills served you pretty well this afternoon. Am I right? Despite your horrible skills with research, were you able to find anything of note, as you slaved over the files all afternoon?"

He was mocking her, she was pretty sure, and she would have bristled except for the fact that—to be fair—she had set herself up to be mocked.

"On our records? Not a lot. We've only computerized in the past couple of years. The rest was paper files, and I have the cuts to prove it.

"Seven of the cats adopted out in the past year specified a spotted pattern, and another eleven were tabbies who might have been spotted or striped, I don't know. I went back five years, and found another couple of hundred cats who might have matched. Not one hundred. Not three. *Five* hundred cats."

"I get the message. I'm buying. Any pattern?"

"Nothing. No particular time of year, no particular type of adopter—not even a gender pattern, which is weird, because usually women and men have different preferences."

"Really?" He considered that for a moment, and then waved the thought away. "Path for another hike. So that's a dead end. Sorry I made you go through all that."

He won points for the apology. "Don't know until you try, right? I did a little online research, though, too. I don't have—what does Nancy call it?—good Google-fu, yeah. But I found some interesting details about cat sacrifices. Did you know that very few magic rituals use animal sacrifice, traditionally?"

Patrick nodded. "Yeah. Animals were too valuable to sacrifice, especially in agrarian cultures. Which also increased the value of one that *was* sacrificed, because it would be without blemish, et cetera, et cetera." He rattled the facts off with ease. "Same with the calves sacrificed in the old Temple in Jerusalem."

She stared at him until he shifted in his seat. 'I know, it's weird stuff to know. My job, it pays to pick up whatever information you can. You never know when it might connect with something else, make random facts into a working hypothesis. I know how to put together a hot tub, sharpen an ax, tat lace—yes, really, and no it doesn't disturb my masculinity at all, thank you very much—and make paper in theory, anyway."

"Right." She was not going to laugh, even though his expression invited her to mock him. She was too aggravated to be amused. "Why did I even bother again?"

"Because you had a thought." He got serious once more. "An idea, a suspicion. That's good, run with it. I trust your brain. What I know and what there is to know are a portion and a whole, and the whole is far greater than the portion could ever aspire to."

She felt her lips finally twitch into a smile despite her annoyance. "What fortune cookie did you get that from?"

"After-dinner mints at Master Li's House of Chili in D.C.. Don't laugh, he makes a mean five-alarm vegetarian chili."

The trouble was, Lily was mostly sure that he was joking, but not *entirely* sure.

He let out a sigh and placed his hands flat down on the table, a gesture of surrender. "Honestly? Anything you think of, anything you see or wonder about… I needed your take on all this. Yeah, I'm the pro. But I never discount a talented amateur's abilities, especially if I can make use of them. You downplay your connection to the cats—fine. Whatever keeps you sleeping at night. But it exists, which means that there might also be a connection we can exploit with our unsub, and his fascination with or need for cats."

Lily was taken aback by his words, both the bluntness and the honesty. "I really, really don't like that thought. At all. About the connection between me and him, I mean."

"I didn't…" Patrick seemed to flounder for a moment. "I didn't mean it that way."

Maybe not, she thought but didn't say, maybe not. Or maybe he did, and was waiting to see what her reaction to that might be. He said himself, he'd use anything and anyone. Exactly what she had suspected about him. And yet, his saying it…somehow made it…less of a threat.

"I just meant that you have a better grasp than someone like me on what might be ticking inside a cat that he can hear. Not that—"

He stopped, looked at his hands, and she could practically see him throw that entire line of conversation out the window. "I've found that getting the point of view of someone outside the bureau, someone who hasn't been subjected to all the same meetings and memos and lectures, gives me a better place to start. We don't know everything—we just want to think that we do. The monsters are less scary if you can deconstruct them."

"Are they?" Lily wondered. She didn't think so. A monster you could understand was still a monster.

"Sometimes. For example, your basic Satanist isn't some kind of off-the-wall loon, but a magical theorist. He—or she—believes that there are certain actions and reactions in magic that can be manipulated. That magic is closer to science than religion. It's results-based, not faith oriented. It's all about sympathy…an object acting upon another, through some law of similarity or contagion. Like voudon, with their gris-gris bags and hex dolls."

Lily had no idea whatsoever what he was talking about. Her parents had been gently lapsed Protestants, which meant that her religious education hadn't ever really happened, and she had never gone through the kind of witchcraft-is-cool phase so many teenage girls seemed to. She'd never been particularly spiritual at all; the woo-woo never wooed her. But at least they weren't talking about her anymore.

"So why do crazies like this sort of magic theory?" she asked, honestly intrigued with the turn of the conversation.

Patrick considered her question, his gaze going sort of hazy, as though he was looking inside his brain. She watched him, fascinated, almost able to hear the gears turning.

"Order. Rationale of a sort that does not depend on the logic we consider, well, logical. If a miracle can occur because God wishes it to occur, because we implore God enough to make it so… Or, conversely and depending on the brand of crazy, if the universe may be influenced significantly by the sheer force of their will—"

"Or sacrifice," she said, bringing the conversation back out of theory and into the reality of their case.

Their case. Lily wasn't sure she liked the taste of that, any more than she liked being told that she was connected in any way, shape or form to the guy Petrosian was looking for. But it felt right. She was involved, from seeing the cats so tenderly, cruelly murdered, to hearing Patrick's thoughts. It felt…personal.

"Yeah. Or sacrifice. I've seen so many kinds, but cats are almost always the most popular."

Lily moved her silverware, adjusting it carefully on the napkin. Breathe, she told herself. Don't let anything through. Don't let the panic attack through. Because she could feel it rising up in her throat like a bad case of the giggles, only not funny at all.

Cats. Sacrifice. Personal.

The sand was soft and shifting underfoot, cool and granular. A cat's long, soft mmrow *following her as she was dragged away, her arm and shoulder making a furrow behind her.*

Breathe. Breathe, and be still.

Patrick didn't seem to notice her distress. "Cats, although traditionally it's black cats, would imply on the surface some kind of pseudosatanic thing. It all depends on if he's using some sort of religious-based ritual, or a purely magical one. Or one that he's making up, based on his own internal rationale." His gaze refocused on her. "That's the theory, anyway."

"Of course, there's another possibility," she said, finally breaking free of the too-vibrant images.

"Oh?" He looked up at her, his head cocked as though what she was about to say was the most important thing he had ever heard.

"This guy may just be crazy."

Patrick's entire face twitched, and before she could react, his entire body was swooping forward, his hand coming up to capture the curve of her jaw, and he had kissed her, swiftly but firmly, on the mouth.

His lips were warm, strong, and tasted ever so slightly of coffee. It wasn't an unpleasant kiss; nor was it a particularly passionate one. It said, clearly, "You delight me and I want to touch you," but didn't go any further over the line than that, and then he was back in position, his body as casually at ease as before.

And they looked at each other, her eyes widened with shock, his heavy lidded, watching her reaction.

"Why did you do that?" she asked, less shocked than bemused. Her lips practically tingled.

"Because I couldn't not." He swallowed, his Adam's apple jolting in his throat. Like his uncharming moments, she found that disturbingly appealing.

But she was solid, steady-as-she-goes Lily. She didn't jump into anything feet-first, not even after she'd measured the depth and tested the waters.

So she waited until he leaned forward again and touched those soft, coffee-scented lips to hers again.

Only then did she let her hands lift to touch the back of his head, stroking the surprisingly soft curls there, curving her fingers around the shape of his skull as she adjusted their angle for better contact.

He let her. She appreciated that. Agent Jon T. Patrick might be arrogant, aggressive and far too focused on the finish line, but he knew a thing or two about letting others take the lead.

Then his mouth opened, teeth capturing her bottom lip gently before his hands were around her neck, thumbs resting against her cheekbones, and Lily suddenly felt as though she were falling endlessly into a velvet-lined pit, the most fabulous room spins ever not brought on by alcohol.

They broke apart. "Oh." It was barely a breath, falling out of Lily's mouth as she tried to recover. She could feel a flush rising up her neck and around down to her breasts. Was that where "hot under the collar" came from?

"We got more than chemistry, Ms. Lily Malkin," he said, shaking his head almost imperceptibly. "We got alchemy."

Something about the words, the way he said them, or the sound of them, made Lily blink. The flush didn't recede, exactly, but the rest of her came back to room temperature.

"You're as dangerous as the people you chase, Agent Patrick," she told him.

"And you're not the kind of woman who would invite me back to her place to continue this discussion out of the range of innocent civilians, are you?"

No. As a profiler, he was right on target. She wasn't.

She very much wished she was, though.

Chapter 7

"Oh man, oh man, oh man." Lily replayed that kiss all the way home; as she brushed her teeth; as she slipped on her nightshirt and toed off her socks; as she crawled into bed and fluffed the pillow; as she flipped channels until, finally, still muttering under her breath, she fell asleep.

And then, she didn't dream of that kiss at all.

"My love." She brought the news to him as a gift, the proof of her devotion. "I have done as you asked of me."

"Have you now?"

His voice was lazy, oiled and smooth like his skin, and she paused in the doorway, suddenly uncertain.

"My love?" Her heart thumped irregularly, as though a dove were trapped within. Something was

wrong. Had she failed somehow? Had her efforts not been enough? She lived in terror of failing him, of seeing the light in his eyes fade, change from love to scorn, or worse, to indifference.

"Have you done all that I required?" he asked her.

"I have." And at great cost to herself; cost she could not allow herself to acknowledge. Pain she would not admit, even as it cut at her heart, crippled her ka, her inner soul. She could not doubt her heart now. He was worth it, worth all she had given up. All she had done, in his name.

"There are none that might stand in your way now."

"There is still one," he disagreed.

"My love?" Even now she could not use his name, could not risk identifying him to a jealous ear, a lingering spy. She cupped the heavy bronze medallion that hung around her neck with one shaking hand. The comfort it normally bought her was absent, and in its place, an unease.

A sleek golden cat turned the corner, turned its head and looked at her, its large luminescent eyes watching her. She reached for it, and it disappeared.

Her lover rose from his chair, bronze skin glinting in the torchlight, muscles moving smoothly. She feasted herself on him, on his beauty, his strength, and the cat was forgotten.

In her distraction a shadow came from the wall behind her where nothing should have been, movement sudden and unexpected. She turned, confused. Pain, like a cobra's strike, bit into her side even as her lover came up to her.

She fell, still clutching the medallion, staring at his beloved face, even as blood and dust filled her mouth.

Why? The question filled her. Why, after all she had done?

"*There is nothing more you may give me,*" *he said almost kindly, as the assassin took the medallion from her stiffening hands.* "*Nothing, save your death. The body of the betrayer will earn me much acclaim with the pharaoh.*"

Love turned to realization, and then to rage, too late as he accepted the medallion from her killer's hands. I will never forgive you, she vowed. I will never forgive myself.

Her ka *shuddered, and slipped out of her body. It paused for a moment, touching her cooling skin with small white paws, then raised its head to the sky and cried for her shame.*

Not forever. Only until you learn to forgive.

Lily sat upright in bed, her heart racing, her skin coated with sweat. The old T-shirt she slept in, the sleeves and collar cut away, clung to her, and she pulled it off in disgust, preferring the cool night air to having the cloth touch her skin an instant longer. She wiped at the sweat, and a shudder wracked her body. "Oh, God."

Another nightmare. That was two in one week, which was two too many, even for her. They were getting worse, not better.

Had this one been about cats again? She didn't think so, but she couldn't remember. There were no details, just a sense of…anger. Betrayal. Sadness.

Lilly pulled up the blanket to cover herself. She lay on her back for a while, then rolled over, shoving a pillow away as though it were to blame for the feeling of suffocation, like something were pressing against her face. The air smelled sour, sweet and warm; too thick, too filled with odors she couldn't quite recognize, as though she had fallen asleep in a stranger's kitchen.

Her mouth opened slightly, her lips pulling back from her teeth as she took in short breaths, as though sipping the air. She realized suddenly that she was trying to taste the air the way cats did, and her laughter conflicted with the business of breathing, making her cough.

"Ugh."

Her entire mouth felt weird, icky, as if she had eaten something nasty, or had had too much to drink.

She hadn't, had she? Lily reclaimed the pillow and shoved it under her head, then gave up and rolled onto her back again. She stared up at the ceiling, thinking over the night.

No. She'd had two beers, well within even her limited abilities. Nothing she hadn't had before, foodwise, and it had all tasted fine. She had gotten home at a reasonable hour…. Jon had followed her home in his newly acquired rental car, against her protests, waiting in his car until she had driven into her condo's garage, gone inside and flicked the porch light at him.

Ridiculous. But she admitted to a faint glow at his concern nonetheless. She had spent her entire adult life looking out for herself. It was nice, even if just for one night, to feel that kind of concern from someone else.

"Don't get too used to it, Lily Malkin," she said sternly. "Mr. FBI made it clear he had career plans. You don't get far with those sort of goals in Newfield."

"Field profilers don't get considered for management slots," he had said over taquitos and Dos Equis. "We're too valuable…so they use us until we're used up. And then we go write books about the experience, see if we can con some new kids into picking up the skills to replace us, start the cycle all over again. I'm not interested in that."

"You *want* a desk job?" It seemed impossible to imagine, an FBI agent bored with what he did.

"I want the ability to actually make a difference on more than a case-by-case basis. Make policy, make changes. And to do that, you need power."

He had grinned then, that surprisingly boyish expression that wiped the intensity from his face and lightened the mood, and they had moved on to another topic of conversation that had nothing to do with the case, his job or cats. The rest of the evening had touched on football, politics, their birth order—she was an only child, he was the youngest of four—and other topics that could have passed for first-date small talk.

And then, outside the restaurant, she had broken their unspoken truce, leaning in to touch her lips to his again.

Sparks. Sparks, and more. Lava.

She had pulled away immediately, and he had let her, not saying a word. But his dark eyes had been knowing. And amused.

"Gah," she said now, no more eloquent on the subject than she had been at the time. What was it about that man?

She was about to roll over yet again and try to get back to sleep, when the alarm clock went off. Already? She looked at the readout and realized that she must have fallen asleep for a few hours without realizing it—it was 6:00 a.m.

The temptation to lie in bed for another hour warred with routine. Routine won. Throwing off the blankets with no grace or dignity at all, Lily grabbed her sweatpants off the chair and staggered to the bathroom to become vaguely human.

Ten minutes later, she was outside her condo, dressed in black fleece sweatpants and a red-and-black hoodie, stretching out cranky muscles before she asked them to work. Her arms over her head, feeling the muscles pull in her back, she could practically feel everything from her heels to her ears align, like a cat stretching after a nap. She tilted her head to better take in the morning air, so much fresher and more interesting than the air inside the building.

She realized as she did so that she was pulling her lips back again, displaying the classic feline grimace as she tasted the air.

"Nancy was right. You need to hang out with people more, if you're picking up habits from the *cats*."

Finishing her stretches, Lily pulled her hair into a ponytail and secured it with a scrunchie, made sure that her sneakers were tied and set off down the street. Three miles, down to the park and back, four times a week, and she had a chance at keeping her hips inside her size eights.

She wondered, as she started to catch the rhythm of her footfalls on the pavement, if Jon was one of those guys who liked his women sleek, or if he had a thing about ribs and hipbones showing.

"Lily Marie, you get your mind out of the gutter," she scolded herself, trying not to laugh as she crossed the street and headed into the park proper. Either she wasn't interested in the guy, or she needed to jump him, but she had to stop wavering between the two.

And if she was going to do the latter, she needed to do it soon. He had gotten all the information available off the scene, and all the facts out of her brain; there was no reason for him to stick around on the taxpayers' dime anymore. He'd be going home soon.

But he promised to find the guy. He promised.

The practical portion of her brain—the majority of it—warned the smaller voice: *Not everyone can keep their promises. Even when they want to.*

And he won't stop working on it, even when he goes home. He won't. He won't. The words worked their way into the slap-slap of shoes on pavement. *He won't. He won't forget.*

The one thing she was certain of, although she could never have said why, or what drove that confidence: *He'll catch the guy. He'll make sure he doesn't hurt anyone ever again.*

The trees were black. The leaves were silver and gray. He remembered, once, the leaves being colored. They had faded slowly, until he could not remember what that color had been. Three years ago? Less. No warning, just a click in his head, like magnets coming together. Sometimes he could almost remember who he had been, before the wake-up call came, and he awoke into this dream. Sometimes, but it was so very difficult, and so very long ago.

He tried not to think about it. It hurt when he did anything other than focus on the ritual, and what he needed to do.

He had been wandering since before the sun rose, searching. He needed to find beasts. Seven beasts, and he only had four. They needed to be right, but he had no more time to breed the perfect ones, and the shelter had said they had no more proper ones to adopt. He could leave his name and number, and they would call him when one came in. But the question smelled cold, and he had hung up without responding.

They would try to stop him. They did not understand.

He would find what he needed. He would hunt them, as they hunted, in the between-hours. In the between-places.

Among the trees would be good. They sometimes could be found living in between the houses and the park, where food was plentiful from picnics and mice. Three more. Four and three would be seven. Seven should be the number. Seven, minus the four he had…

Something tugged at his awareness. There. Over there.

His thoughts scattered. Distracted from his numbers, but why? What…

A flash. Like a bird flitting from branch to branch, only at street level.

A woman, waiting at the corner for the light to change.

Gold. She was hammered gold, gilded like a statue.

His brain caught up with his fancy, and he was able to focus better on her.

No, she wasn't gold. She was flesh and shadows, the same as all the rest. But he saw the glints in her, shimmering and shiny. Bright and sharp, moving quickly down the sidewalk, across the street from him. Into the trees.

Like the beasts.

It was Her.

No. His heart stuttered back down into a normal beat. It was just a woman, a normal woman. A mortal, human woman.

Beasts, he reminded himself. He was on a mission to find the beasts he needed. Not a woman. But he couldn't look away from her as she moved away from him, moving away. Golden, glowing like fire. He felt himself yearning toward it, as though it would warm him the way the gray sun no longer did. The way his dreams, filled with heat and wind, told him he had once been warm.

She was important. She could be… Her, come to this world? One of Her handmaidens, perhaps, lost the same way he was?

Yes. *Yes.* Something inside him thrilled to the re-alization.

He took a step toward the curb, intending to cross the street and follow her, when something yanked him back, as though strings were attached to his knees and elbows. The clarity of her warmth was suddenly clouded by apprehension, the appeal matched by an equal resistance. Important, but wrong. Dangerous.

No! The first warmth he had felt in so long, the first true connection to Her. He would not let it go.

Forcing himself forward, he followed the woman. Into the trees, down a path laid with dirt. She moved swiftly but with a steady pace; graceful, a predator on the hunt. Unable to do more than walk quickly without attracting attention, he was about to lose her, when suddenly she stopped.

What had stopped her? He drew to the side of the path, watching as she knelt. To tie her shoe? No.

A beast approached her. He jerked forward, instinctively ready to grab the beast, but it was not the right sort: red as clay, and useless to him. The revulsion he felt in the presence of the beasts overwhelmed him once the instinct fled, even with the amulet to protect him. He fought the urge to flee, to snatch the glowing woman away from the foul thing and destroy it before it could befoul her as well.

But the woman gestured, and the beast made obeisance as much as any beast ever could; tail erect and head forward, sniffing her proffered hand until it stroked its fur.

Something hurt inside, like a knife prying open a seal, and he stayed where he was, even as she rose from the beast and began moving again.

She confused him. She was beloved of the beasts, and therefore anathema to him. And yet, She was the most beloved of the beasts, wasn't She? So this woman was a link, a true link.

And yet, the woman was also part of the danger he had sensed. Women like that were not to be trusted. They were to be removed, offered up to the greater goal, before they could confuse people, tell lies….

And yet, he was drawn to her. Needed her. The confusion bothered him. Worried him. He had to know why she alone had color and warmth, the same warmth his dreams promised him, if he could do this one thing….

He hit his forehead with the heels of his hands, willing his brain to stop whirling. He had no room, no time for confusion. He knew what he had to do. A female had no place in his goals, what he must accomplish. Especially not a best-beloved of the beasts. Seven beasts, proper beasts, three yet to be found…

Yet, if he could find an answer in her…

Perhaps he would not need the beasts, after all.

But he waited too long to decide. She was gone.

No. His head ached, but he was calm once again. She was a mirage, a taunt. The gold he had seen was a phantasm, a delusion. He would continue with his plan.

Chapter 8

"Yes, sir."

Patrick paused in the middle of his note taking and twirled his pen, stretching his legs in front of him, wincing as his half-asleep leg twinged in protest. The narrow windowsill on the stairwell landing was not exactly suited to a tall man perching there for any length of time, but it was the only place in the warren of the police station where his cell phone could actually get reception. The bureau got pissy when agents were out of touch for very long; the fact that the entire country wasn't wired for perfect cell reception didn't seem to have sunk in to the powers that be in Washington.

"Yes, sir. I'm wrapping up my notes now. Yes, sir, I expect to be on a plane tomorrow morning. My report will be on your desk as soon as I'm in the office. Yes, sir. No, sir, I don't believe this was—"

A shadow fell over him, and he looked up.

Petrosian, looking like the Doom of Gloom in rumpled flesh.

"Hang up."

Patrick made a gesture to indicate the fact that he couldn't do that. Hanging up on your direct supervisor was bad form. Not that he hadn't done it a time or three. Or four. He needed more reason than a cranky cop to do it, though.

"Hang up," Petrosian repeated. "We got another."

"Change of plans," he said into the phone, already standing and reaching with his free hand for his coat. "Another incident. I'll check in later. Don't wait up, don't hold dinner."

His boss, used to him after seven years, merely grunted assent, and hung up, doubtless already dialing another field agent to ream out for some cause or another.

"What do we know?" he asked the detective, tucking the phone into his pocket and following him through the hallways. Already his brain was sorting through the known facts, clearing way for new information.

"Not a lot. Some guy had a bunch of cats snatched from his cattery—he's a breeder, down by Mazelle Park. Spotted cats," he added, as though Patrick was too slow to figure that bit out for himself. "Some kind of special breed. Thief took only males, not a surprise. Uniform got a pretty decent description of the guy off the security cameras, so we can distribute it. Our first real damn break in this damn case."

"How long ago?"

"The incident? Yesterday. We got news of it about three hours ago, more or less. The call went through animal welfare, and once they got a confirmation and checked it out they sent it on to us, and someone had to come find me."

"Yesterday? And then it took them three hours to find you?" Jesus, what was with this podunk police department? He should have been informed immediately! If they had a description of this guy on file already…

Patrick felt himself literally getting hot under the collar, and pulled it down a notch. Petrosian made a weary-looking shrug as he held the door to the parking garage open for the agent. "Whaddaya want me to say? Not everyone reads their memos."

The detective was right: there was no way everyone could have known to contact Petrosian just for a cat-napping. He knew as well as anyone how departments didn't talk to each other. "So we're checking this guy out? Or do we have—"

"That's where it gets interesting. We found the cats, yeah. Our boy's been busy."

That didn't sound good at all.

By the time they got to the site, halfway across town in the opposite direction from the first three locations, Patrick had managed to start up a new page in his log-book for this incident, listing what little Petrosian had been able to give him, factswise. He had only the existing police reports on the first two; it would be important to see firsthand how similar—or not—this scene was to the one he had checked out. His notes were his usual precise and factual work, without any of his own personal interpretation—those went on another sheet, to keep them separate and not confuse the issue. He also had a pencil sketch of the suspect to go with the sketch the artist had done from Lily's observations and extrapolations. All of which led up to…nothing. So far. The guy was careful, a planner. He—or she, don't make assumptions, he cautioned himself—was working toward something, a something only he—or she—knew about.

But things were turning. Patrick could feel it. To actually steal cats, in full view, suggested desperation, and desperation led to mistakes.

It also, he knew, often led to increased violence. His theories aside, they had to stop this guy before he— she—screw it, *he* escalated. Before any humans got caught up in this guy's fantasies.

"Oh great gobs of hell." Petrosian pulled the unmarked sedan to the curb and swore in disgust, making Patrick look up. In addition to the three patrol cars marking off the area, there were two vans. Even if they hadn't had the markings of the two local news stations on the side panels, the antenna rig on the roof of each gave the game away.

"The vultures have arrived," Patrick said. "Damn them. Can you keep them off the scene?"

"I'll do what I can," Petrosian said. "You go on around; I'll draw their fire up front."

Good man, Petrosian. He could see why Lily liked the cop. The fact that the guy was old enough to be Lily's dad, and looked like a particularly tired, overweight hound made Patrick inclined to like him even more.

The older cop stalked toward the flashing lights and cameras, waving his arms to catch their attention. "People! People, behind the tape, thank you very much. Geordie, come on, you know the damn drill, back behind the tape!"

While the detective corralled the news crews and started to feed them some line promising a full accounting of whatever dire disaster they were claiming this was—it had to be a slow news day, or these were the scrub teams sent out for filler—Patrick moved up the sidewalk toward the alley where two uniforms were talking to an older man with a grimy white apron tied over jeans and a sweatshirt.

"Yeah, I heard him down there, and I seen him in the mornings. I dunno, he looked like a guy, ya know? Don't bother me, go find the guy!"

The witness sounded as though he had watched too many episodes of *Law & Order,* Patrick thought as he came even with them. The agent wasn't much of a linguist, but the coarse accent seemed horribly out of place here in far more proper Newfield. Even Lily's West Coast lilt had been worn down over the years by the granite of New England into more of a drawl.

"Sir, if you would please answer the questions, that would be a great help." The cop was clearly out of patience. Patrick could relate.

"What do we have here?" He hated flashing his badge, but this wasn't his scene and Petrosian wasn't here to vouch for him.

The senior of the two cops answered him, after scanning the badge and deciding he had a right to be there asking questions. "Roger Hooperman. Owns the store next door."

"Not the owner of any of the stolen cats?" That guy was probably busy with insurance forms and client calls.

"Nope. I'm the guy as found 'em." Hooperman was clearly glad for a new, hopefully more appreciative audience. "Sick bastard, whoever done that. I got nothing against animals, ya know. They're fine, and a cat as is a mouser is a damn good thing to have, ya know? But they're just animals. I don't got nothing sentimental about them. But what that guy done, that's just wrong." Hooperman shook his head, the image of outraged citizenry.

The second officer gestured into the alleyway. "There's a door there, leads down to the basement. The door was open when Mr. Hooperman came out, and he—"

"I smelled 'em. Used to work in a butcher shop, I know the smell of meat."

"And you called the cops?" Patrick tried to keep his voice neutral, but his disbelief came through. Even the most upstanding of citizens didn't call out the cops for a whiff of spoiled meat.

"Nah, man, not until I saw it." Hooperman lost none of his bravado. "Saw what that guy'd done."

"And then you called the cops."

"Damn straight."

"Was that before or after you called the local television stations and informed them that you'd found evidence of a satanic cult in Newfield?"

The cops looked startled, but Hooperman simply

shrugged. "Hey, news is news." If he was even remotely embarrassed by his actions, he hid it like a pro.

Patrick had stopped being amazed by what people would do for publicity. "And your face and storefront in the news can only mean curious people coming by, which means business."

Hooperman kept his cool, even in the face of the agent's scorn. "Got it in one. But that guy, he's still scum. You'll find him."

That was the second time since arriving in Newfield that someone had said those words to him. He was used to being told to solve cases, find killers. But the words echoed with him oddly as he walked down the narrow stairwell, the smell of cat piss and bleach almost overwhelming the stink Hooperman had mentioned. Patrick didn't believe in fate, karma or predestination. But this case was almost designed for his skills, designed to bring him to this town, to this place, these players.

"And bring you to this specific basement? Get a grip, Jon T.," he told himself, then stopped, both his speech and his steps.

You had to know what you were looking for to smell it. But once you knew, there was no way to ignore it.

"Damn." He pushed open the door, already knowing what he would find.

The setup was almost exactly as the last one: a room filled with makeshift metal cages—fewer this time, and smaller—and another room with a black drape on the floor, seven limp bodies arranged nose to tail.

He knelt and inspected the bodies without touching

them. They were fresh—the time between the killings was definitely getting shorter. Not a good sign. But all the details were wrong, just as he'd said to Lily. This guy wasn't playing by the usual rules. He had some other game in mind. But what? He needed to get inside this guy's motivations, to figure out what had triggered the killing, what was driving him to such extremes, to breed his own victims and set up such careful scenes.

Patrick recognized Petrosian's tread on the stairs behind him, the walk heavy without sounding lumbering or awkward.

"The cuts are more jagged," the agent said without rising from his crouch over the grisly display. "He wasn't being as precise. Maybe rushed. Or nervous."

"Or the kitties were giving him trouble? Because that's been bothering me. How does he get them so calm?" Petrosian moved around to face Patrick, looking down at the bodies. "Tox came back. None of the cats so far have been drugged. When I try to clip my cats' claws, they put up a fight. But these…they just lay there and let him do it, one after the other?"

Patrick stared at the bodies. That was a good question. A damn good question. And, short of drugs, or restraints—neither of which were showing up at the scene or coming up on the toxicology screens, he could only come up with one answer. "Lily could do it, based on what you've said. Maybe we've got another cat talker on our hands."

"Jesus." Petrosian didn't sound happy. Good. Patrick wasn't happy either. He wanted to see Lily again, yeah, but not like this. Not over the bodies of more dead moggies. Not with her thinking about someone with her skill doing this. He selfishly wanted her relaxed, soft, not tense or worried.

But the job came first, last and always.

He pulled out his cell phone and dialed the number he'd already memorized.

"This is Lily. Leave a message."

Despite himself, he was amused. Short and to the point, just like the woman herself. Nothing in the voice even suggested the way she smelled, sun-warmed even on a cool evening, or the way she felt, sparks and shivers under his lips. Or the way she made blood rush from his brain to his groin in a manner definitely unbecoming to a federal agent on the case.

"It's Jon. Agent Patrick. Call me."

Nothing of what he really wanted to say. No time for that, not now.

The bar was wide but not very deep, and there were too many people crowded together. The news droned in the background, a woman with a microphone and a stylish wool coat, standing in a run-down part of town. Red lights flashed against the gray concrete walls, and the yellow stretch of tape kept people out of the alley between two buildings

The phone was in the back, near the bathrooms, and it was quieter there, nobody lingering to use the johns. The phone's receiver was cold in his hand, the plastic odd feeling and wrongly shaped. He hadn't wanted to call in the place he lived. He had gotten the number off the computer at home, written it down and walked with it in his hand until he came in here on a whim.

One ring. Two, and someone on the other end picked up before the ring was completed. When a woman answered, he closed his eyes and spoke clearly, calmly, with the proper enunciation. The language felt strange in his mouth, his brain wanting to use other words, but he forced his way through.

He had to be heard. They had to understand.

"You don't understand. I'm not dangerous. They should just leave me alone. I only want what's mine."

"Sir?" A clicking noise, and he was transferred, almost immediately. He could almost feel himself racing through the wires, up and down the building, until finally landing in the proper department, with the right person to hear him.

That was what it took; knowing how to make the right people hear you.

"Talk to me." A man's voice this time, commanding in a way that thrilled him with fear. He could almost see them scurrying around, waving their arms and trying to trace his call. It didn't matter. He would be gone soon. He would win this time.

"Tell your warriors to hold off. The Serpent hunting in the night does not wish to strike. It desires only to return to its home. To be safe and warm and dry, away from the talons of the hawk, the claws of the hunting cat. It will not strike unless cornered."

A cough, the sound of chairs pushing away from desks in the background. He had keen hearing, and he heard all, alert to every nuance, every dip and change.

"Are you telling us you are no danger? Are you the Night Serpent?"

"It is as good a name as any." He preferred talking to a woman; women understood things that needed to be done. Women understood that power ebbed and flowed, came and went, that it needed to be coaxed, cajoled before it would respond. They did not waste time naming things, but went to the heart of them. They had always been the heart of power.

Women. Woman. The woman he had seen. Maybe he had been wrong to dismiss her. She was golden, filled with life, where all others were gray and unreal. She had power there, inside. Golden shining power, sun and sand, not the drab of this world. Maybe the power he needed. If he could find her again, she would be able to tell him what to do, what he was doing wrong.

"The cat woman. She knows. She knows."

He had only meant to say it to himself. He didn't realize until the man repeated it, that the words had been said out loud.

"Knows what? Sir, if you'll talk to me, I can help you."

They had no idea who he was. He had wanted to reassure them, let them know that he would not bother them, so long as they left him be. But he knew now that it couldn't be. Just as before…

Before when?

In the place where he had been warm. Powerful. Before they had cast him down and thrown him away, sent him to this dreary place.

Everything was smaller here. Colder. Worn down.

He was confused again. But he knew where he had gone wrong.

"Sir, talk to me."

There was only way back to what had been. He needed power, yes. The woman *had* shown him, simply by her being. By the way the beasts responded to her. The beasts would bring him what he needed…but he needed beasts of the old world, not this cold new one, this suddenly unfamiliar one. He needed beasts who felt the taste of that golden shining in them. He needed to set that free, bathe in it, become it. Only then would he find his way home.

He hung up the phone carefully, the man still speaking on the other end, and walked through the crowd, out the front door and into the cool night air.

Yes. Oh, yes. He was on his way now.

Chapter 9

Lily came home from work to find a familiar unmarked police car sitting in front of her condo. "Damn it." All she wanted was to get through life without a fuss, without drama or trauma. Having cops staking out her home did not qualify under any of those headings, especially if the neighbors caught wind of it.

She probably should have called Jon when he left a message, but she'd not been sleeping well, and the thought of having to deal with him—or, worse, more of the case—pushed her over the line from exhausted to unable to deal. So she had left the message, undeleted, on her machine, and pretended it didn't exist.

Piper had come to be paid.

She pulled past them and into her driveway, leaving the garage door open so that they could join her.

"Gentlemen," she said. She was too tired for this; as much as the sight of her Fibbie, almost as rumpled as Aggie now, with his tie slightly askew, made her want to smile, she really just wanted to fall over on the sofa and cry herself to sleep. Except sleep wasn't such a good thing these days, because every time she closed her eyes she saw a dignified cat sitting there, tawny coat glimmering, green eyes glinting at her as though expecting her to do something brilliant, wonderful, heroic, and save him.

"I need coffee," Aggie said. "And so do you."

Lily tried to dig in her heels. "What happened?"

He shook his head at her. "Coffee first."

So she let them into her home, settled them at the table in the open space that served as a combination dining room/living room and went into the kitchen to brew up a pot of Hawaii's best. It was rare enough that she had company; she had to hunt through the cabinets for three mugs that would do.

"Milk? Sugar?"

Aggie took it fully doctored; Jon only wanted sugar. She fixed the mugs and brought them out, sitting across the table from Jon, next to Aggie. She didn't plan it that way, but having the table between her and him seemed like a good idea.

Until she looked at him and saw that intense gaze fixed on her. Suddenly she wanted Aggie to shut up and go away. And at the same time she was very glad that he was there with them.

Then that gaze flickered off, going from molten to

business cool. "Have you watched the news today?" Jon—Agent Patrick—asked.

"I read the paper this morning, but no. Why?" She turned to look at Aggie, struck by the look in his eyes. It was more than worry or exhaustion. There was… anger there.

He fiddled with his coffee, took a long sip. "Jesus, that's good. Better than the swill at the station."

"Aggie?" She trusted him to tell her the truth. But he merely looked away.

Patrick was the one who started talking. "There was another… We found more cats." The way he said it, she knew they were already dead. "We have a description of the guy who stole them. And we have a possible witness who may be able to identify him in person."

She turned to face him, warming her fingers on her coffee cup. Her hands were cold. Everything was cold. "Oh God, the poor cats. But it's good, right, that you have a witness?"

"It's good, yeah." He didn't sound convinced of that. "But the witness called the media, too. Bad luck for us, it's a slow day. They ran the story on the five-o'clock broadcast."

Lily drank her own coffee, hoping the warmth would spread through her, trying to understand why the publicity would be a bad thing. "He might see it and run?" she guessed. But that didn't explain why they were here, looking so nervous. "Jon? What did they say, on the news?"

He opened his mouth to say something, but couldn't get the words to come out.

"Lily." Petrosian took over again. "It wasn't what was on the news that was the problem. Exactly."

She turned to face Aggie again, feeling a cold curling unease in her belly that not even the warmest coffee could ward off. "What?"

"The guy? The killer, or someone who claimed to be him? He called the local station. The television station. After they ran the clip. He's crazy, or making a good show of it, but—"

Patrick interrupted Aggie's ramblings, finally managing to get to the point. "Lily, he mentioned you."

"What?" The cold abandoned her belly and went right up her spine, freezing her brain.

"Not by name," Aggie reassured her, putting his coffee down to reach over and pat her hand awkwardly. "But he definitely mentioned a cat lady. And who else could it be but you?"

"But…how? And why?"

Patrick slumped in his chair, for the first time since she had met him giving up entirely on the "agent in charge" arrogance. That scared her more than anything else. "I don't know. Maybe he adopted—or tried to adopt—a cat from your shelter and heard about you? Or, if he watches the news, which he seems to, maybe he's seen you on TV before, and somehow got you tangled up in whatever he's trying to do? Maybe, if he's a local boy.

"Christ. I don't even know that, maybe your coming here was what triggered him, or… The fact that he only started recently doesn't mean he just got here, he could have done this before our three-year mark, too. And if that's true, then the trigger could be anything."

He sighed, rubbing a hand over his face. "I haven't been able to get a fix on what he wants, or where he's coming from. I don't have anything yet."

He suddenly seemed to remember who he was talking to and straightened in his chair. "But I'm working on it," he promised her. "We know more than we did before. I have a call in to the bureau—he didn't make any direct threats against you, but the fact that you've been brought in even by implication raises the case's priority from animal to human threat."

Lily wasn't sure that made her feel much better. Not that she didn't trust him, it was just…the witness must be useless, otherwise they'd already be arresting the guy—the unsub was the term, right? They wouldn't be sitting here at her table drinking coffee and looking worried. If they didn't know who he was, or why he was doing this, or what had made him focus on her, how could they stop him? How could they even find him?

I can't help you, kitten, she whispered to the waiting cat of her dreams. *I'm not even sure how to help myself.*

"You shouldn't go back to the shelter," Aggie said.

"Excuse me?" That had the ability to shake her out of her thoughts.

The older man leaned on the table, his houndlike face full of earnest concern. "Lily, this guy, okay so maybe he hasn't hurt any humans yet. Yet. And what he said, it wasn't a threat. But I don't like him even knowing you exist. If he found out about you through the shelter, then that's where he's going to be looking. And no matter what J. Edgar here says, we can't spare someone to follow you around just on the off chance that this guy might actually be dangerous. You know that. So staying away from where he might look for you only makes sense."

Lily scowled into her coffee. It might make sense. But the thought of not being allowed to go to the shelter, not to be able to handle the new kittens so that they became used to humans; not to see the older cats as they came out of their shyness and started interacting, to be away from the soothing smells and sounds…

And then she had to laugh at herself. When did cats become comfort to her?

"Lily." Aggie was still talking. "And even if we manage to keep a lid on what he said, which I doubt, the media's gonna show up at the shelter soon too. Cats have been slaughtered, and Felidae No-Kill is the best game in town for publicity hounds. They'll want a sound bite, and they'll probably want it from you. And if somebody puts the pieces together, which they're smart enough to do…"

"What's to stop them from coming here?" she asked.

"This is private property. They can camp outside, but they can't harass you, or I get to come over and harass them in return." Aggie looked almost happy at that thought, and Lily felt herself smile a little in return. He so badly wanted—needed—to do *something*.

"You should take a leave of absence from work, as well," Patrick said, breaking into the moment.

"What?" Lily felt her hackles rise up. "I can't do that." Mr. FBI might be able to take time off on a whim, but she had bills to pay. And it wasn't as though there was anyone who could just step in and take over for her; they were shorthanded already. And—

"Lily, don't be an idiot," Jon said sharply.

"Excuse me?" Her gaze met his, ice cold to burning hot. As hard as he pushed her physical buttons he could nail the emotional ones too, apparently. She felt the urge to arch her back and hiss at him.

Aggie put his coffee down and pushed his chair away. "Children, play nice. I have to get back to the station. Patrick, you coming back with me?" The implication in his voice was that Agent Patrick should say yes, and leave Lily alone to deal with her own decisions. Jon, however, wasn't listening, still holding her gaze with his own.

"I'll be fine. I can call a cab. Go on."

Petrosian shrugged, abandoning them to their own fates. He wasn't fool enough to put his hand into a cat-spat, even before the claws actually showed up.

He reached over to pat Lily's hand again, not taking offense when she flinched. "I'll make sure patrol cars up their drive-bys. If anything's even the slightest bit hinky, or you just want them to stop by for some of this damn fine coffee, you let me know, okay?"

"All right. Thank you, Aggie. For everything." She stood up, intending to see him to the door.

"Just doin' my job, ma'am." He grinned at her; it was forced, but she appreciated the effort. "You stay safe, is all I ask. And don't hurt the Fibbie, okay?"

"I'll do my best," she said.

She came back and watched Jon, sitting at her dining-room table, turning the mug of coffee around in his hands. She didn't think he'd even taken a single sip yet. He was more worried than she was, she realized. He was worried about *her.*

The thought raised her internal temperature again, but this time not in anger.

Aggie worried, but he worried because he felt he'd brought all this on her. There was responsibility and guilt wrapped up in his concern. It didn't make the worry any less real, but there was a *reason* for it. This...

Agent Patrick had no reason to worry. He hadn't brought her into it; he hadn't brought this killer to her door. Potentially, she added. Potentially to her door. The news would do that, if it happened, and they had gotten the information from the guy himself, so it wasn't anything Patrick had done or not done....

It struck her suddenly. Jon was worried because there was a risk to her. And risk to her made him worry. It was a closed equation she wasn't used to: someone worried about her simply because they cared.

Something surged in her, thick and unfamiliar, and she tried, instinctively, to force it down. But it was warm, so warm, and part of her yearned for it, allowing it to slip through her body.

Be careful, a voice whispered to her. A thin, cold voice that stopped the warmth in its tracks. *No one is to be trusted.*

Confused and frustrated, she reached for the cold core of practicality that had always ruled her life. But it slid out of her grasp, suddenly distant and difficult to find. She felt the sting of tears, and blinked them away. As she did so, she became aware of a shadow falling over her eyes. Startled, she blinked again. And again. It was slight but clear: something was covering her eye the instant before her lid came down.

The more she focused on it, the more aware she was that her eyesight was strange, too. The colors seemed different: the blues and greens were deeper, while the deep brown tones of her furniture seemed almost gray.

"Jon?"

Her voice sounded strange, too. Oddly pitched, and filled with vibrato and echoes she couldn't recognize.

She must have sounded odd to him as well, because he reacted as though she had yelled, spilling coffee as he jumped out of his chair. The smell of the liquid, suddenly acrid and unpleasant, twitched in her nostrils and made her sneeze.

"Lily, what? Holy shit…" He reached out and touched her chin with his fingers, tipping her head up to look into her eyes.

"What?"

"Your eyes. They're all pupil. Like you OD'd on belladonna or something…."

She blinked again. His eyes were darker than she remembered, and his voice was weird, too. Everything felt strange, as if she was falling, her sense of balance completely gone. She felt the urge to lean against him, and fought it.

"Jon, what's going on? What's happening?" She started to shake.

Down on all fours, stretching. Lacking a tail, she could not mimic the temple cat's actions exactly, but her teacher knew the human was trying, and was patient with her, the way one might with a slow but beloved kitten.

"Miuuuuu. Miuuuu." Thus, silly girl. Thus you bow before Herself, and receive Her regard. The cat was

regal; lean, plush-furred, spotted tawny and black, like the desert itself. Great green eyes watched her, large ears twitching forward, as though to encourage her charge to learn more swiftly....

Then she felt it, rising along her spine, from tail-that-wasn't to whiskers-that-weren't. A sense of connection, of power, of strength that was alien and yet entirely hers...

"*Miauuuu?*" *she essayed, the sound rising from deep within her throat.*

Those ears twitched sharply in approval, and she felt her mouth stretch in a purely human grin in response.

"Lily!"

He was shaking her, and she felt the urge to hiss, to strike at him with hands curved as though...

"Oh." She gasped, her world reeling. "Oh goddess..."

Lily felt her knees give way, and she collapsed into Jon's arms.

There were hands upon her head, ointment upon her brow. The soft touch of claws against her skin.

You are my daughter. I am your mother. We will always be tied to each other, forevermore. Not even your faithlessness will change that....

"Mother, forgive me...."

"Lily?"

The voice was familiar. And it sounded...right. Lily opened her eyes, feeling stickiness gumming her eyelids together briefly, before Patrick's face came into focus over her.

"It's so cold...."

He had a blanket wrapped around her before she

could finish. The intensity of his gaze warmed her almost as much as the fleece, but even as she thought that, a worm of unease crept back. His dark gaze was warm, but…disturbing at the same time. Too much: too focused. Too *wanting*. What did he want from her? Whatever it was, she couldn't do it. She could barely remember her own name right now.

Lily, a voice whispered to her. *Here, now, your name is Lily.*

"Are you all right? You scared the crap out of me, collapsing like that. Did you eat anything today?" He loomed in too close, his voice shaking.

"I'm fine, yes, and back off, will you?" She struggled to sit up, only to find her movement impeded by his hovering. "Come on, Agent Patrick, move. I—"

The sensation of *wrongness* hit her again. Only this time it wasn't wrong, but right, and when it left as suddenly as it swept in, Lily cried out at the loss, the bereftness of it.

Mother, forgive me….

"Lily. Lily, come back to me. Come on, open your eyes, look at me…."

She was in his arms. No, on his lap, cradled against his broad chest the way she might hold a kitten. His hands were warm, even through the fabric of her sweater, and the stroke of them up and down her arm, made her want to purr.

"I'm okay," she said, not moving.

"No. You're not. Lily, what's going on?"

"I don't know," she admitted. It was easier to talk with her face turned against his chest, her hair hiding her from him—and him from her—like some kind of privacy screen. "I keep…I've been having dreams. All week. Dreams… I've always had nightmares, things I didn't remember, but they're worse now. Cats, you know? This one cat, sitting there, staring at me."

"That's…normal. I'm sorry." There was an odd tone in his voice. Guilt? But why would he be guilty?

"No, it's okay." The irony of her reassuring him didn't escape her. "I expected it. You can't see something like that without it going somewhere, we both know that. And I've…" She hesitated. "I've always dreamed of cats." It was true; she was only now allowing herself to remember the depth of it. How the dreams followed her throughout college, becoming worse during times of stress. Especially when she was in a relationship. When a relationship was starting…or ending. But she wasn't going to tell him that. It was just her insecurities taking a classic form, echoing her waking fears. All of her therapists had said so.

"It's not the dreams so much as… The cat I see is alive and…waiting. Looking at me. Expecting me to do something.

"And then this week I was so tired from dreaming, from not sleeping, I…I started hallucinating."

It was easier to call it that. To pretend that it was all just sleep deprivation playing tricks on her mind. Perfectly logical, and easily dealt with, via sleeping pills and a few sessions with a new therapist.

Perfectly logical, and untrue. They weren't hallucinations. They were *real*.

That was impossible. So she had to be losing her

mind. Don't tell Jon that. Don't make him think of her as another crazy, someone to be studied and tracked and analyzed….

"Aw, baby."

If anyone else had called her that, Lily would have taken offense. But it came so easily out of his mouth, without any inflection that might have made it patronizing, or pitying, or insulting. She felt his arms tighten around her, and felt, suddenly as though she could melt into his body; seep into his bones and be safe and warm forever.

He cared for her. She cared for him. She could love him, if he let her.

The thought made her jolt away, as though someone had touched her with a live wire.

Don't trust him. Don't ever trust a man, not ever again.

"Hey." He let her move away, but kept one arm around her, keeping her on his lap. He was warm, so warm. What was she afraid of? Like cats…her own fear was the fearsome thing, not this attraction. This connection.

All it took was a turn of her torso, and they were face-to-face. Her hair came forward in a sheet, and he reached up to brush it back, tucking several of the thick curls behind her ear.

His hand was shaking. She liked that. Control over herself she knew about. Control of someone else…

"Your eyes…they're still dilated." His hand was still resting in her hair. She wondered if he realized that.

"Hrmmm." She could smell him, his arousal. Her mouth watered at the thought of what he might taste like. She already knew his mouth, the texture of his hair, the softness of his neck…. What other surprises might be hidden under that suit and tie?

It had been a while since she'd dated. Longer since then that she'd had sex. She thought that there might still be condoms in the drawer of her night table. They should still be good…. Did they expire? It hadn't been that long, had it?

Her thighs ached with the need to feel his weight between them, feel the heft and warmth of him there, inside her, a part of her. She wanted to feel the scrape of his hands against her skin, his fingers tangling in her hair, his mouth on her neck, her breasts…. She could feel her nipples harden at the thought, and the ache between her thighs turned into a liquid heat.

"What are you thinking?" he asked her, dropping his hand from her hair and bringing her attention back to the here and now.

Instead of answering, she slid her arms around his neck, brought him close and kissed him.

Jon had thought that he would have to be the aggressor, that he would be the one to make the first real move. And probably the second, too. He was okay with that; based on their first, totally unplanned kisses, Lily was clearly gun-shy: someone had done a number on her, probably, and she didn't want to jump into some fly-by-night thing. He liked that. It was frustrating, but he liked it. She wasn't old-fashioned, exactly, just… cautious. Like a cat, she would wait him out.

He was okay with that, too.

Not that he'd worked out any sort of plan in any kind of detail, only vague ideas that kept occurring to him without warning. He would talk to her, let her know he wasn't a bad guy for all that they got off on a bad start. Maybe coax a few more kisses from her, if the situation allowed. No pressure. Wrap up this case and then call her a few days later, when he was home in D.C. His life was crazed; he never knew where he'd be from week to week; federal agents, especially with his specialization, traveled a lot, and without much warning. But that was what cell phones were for, not to mention frequent-flier miles.

All that went out of his head the instant her lips touched his. Icy-hot, sweet-tasting, sliding like silk over his skin, her hands insistent, her hunger obvious. A man would have to have been a saint to resist, and he might have the name of a saint, but that was as far as it went.

"Lily…"

He tried, Lord knew, he tried. She clearly wasn't entirely in control of herself, between the sleep deprivation and the hallucinations and now this…. But it wasn't as though she had been unresponsive to him. He wasn't taking advantage—was he?

She pulled back as though sensing his hesitation, and smiled at him. Her eyes were normal; they were clear, and bright, and very much aware of what she was doing.

That was all the reassurance he needed.

"Lily." He whispered her name just before her mouth came down on his again, nipping the delicate flesh, sliding her tongue along the inside of his lips, tasting and suckling like…like a hummingbird, he thought. Or a cat, lapping cream…

"Get out of those clothes." She was standing, tugging at his shirt. "Too warm in here for clothing." She was smiling, tendrils of her hair, dampened by sweat and tears, were clinging to her neck like invitations to be followed. He reached for the buttons of his shirt, even as he was giving in to temptation and moving his mouth to that spot on her neck, doing some tasting of his own.

"You taste like…honey. Warm honey and whiskey. Ah, Lily." He was lost. He didn't even try to resist.

There was something deeply…sexy about turning a guy on. She had almost forgotten, maybe she had never known; the passion contained in a man who wanted, waiting only permission to take. The seduction was all about drawing out the process, letting him know that it was available but holding off on the go-ahead; knowing that they both knew where it would end, and therefore feeling free to play, to delay, to build the tension to where they were both sweating with the need.

His shirt unbuttoned, she let her fingers run from his shoulders down his chest to his belly, then back up again, close-trimmed nails barely scratching the skin. Dark hair started at his pectorals, covering his chest in a thick mat, then trailing to a narrow line down to his belly button. His body was firm, muscled but not bulky. Solid. He was solid in a way that made her—for the first time in her life—feel delicate.

Lily had no illusions about her body. She was lush. Hourglass-shaped. When she was in her twenties, she finally gave up. Exercise kept her muscles firm, but nothing short of starvation was ever going to give her a flat stomach or slender hips.

"C'mere" he said, his hand sliding down her back, cupping her rear and pulling her to where he sat on the sofa. The blanket he had wrapped around her fell to the floor unnoticed as she returned to his lap, this time for an entirely different purpose than comfort.

He slid his hands under her sweater, stroking the flesh upward, sliding his fingers over the strap of her bra up to her neck, and then down again. She raised her arms and he had her sweater off and tossed it to the floor.

"Fast reflexes," she practically purred.

"Government issue," he said, then his lips were caressing the valley between her breasts, and she *was* purring. His lips were warm, so warm, and greedy. His hands were flat against her back, his tongue soft and wet on her skin, and she felt as if he was drinking her up through her skin.

Her fingers threaded through his hair, suggesting, if not directing, his actions.

"Tell me what you want," he said, the whisper hot against her nipples. "Tell me. Talk dirty to me."

She had never done any such thing, had no idea where to begin.

"It's all right, Lily-kit. Just say what you want. What you want to do to me. I want to lick every inch of you, mouth to toes. Especially your belly. I bet your belly tastes so sweet…"

"I can't…. Hold me. Hold me down."

In the time it took for her to gasp her request, she was flat on her back on the floor, Jon's body looming over hers, her arms stretched over her head and pinned to the floor with one of his hands around her wrists.

"You want to test yourself against me, kitten?" He might call her kitten but he was the one purring, now. A big cat noise, smug and self-satisfied.

No. Yes. She had always been in control. Always been the one to initiate—and to leave. He would be the one to leave, in this relationship. Begin as you mean to go on....

"I won't force you," he promised, lowering his mouth to her breasts again. "But I won't let you go, either."

He was lying. She knew he was lying. But she could pretend, for this one night.

Then his mouth closed down hard on one nipple, and her back arched up, her legs closing around his and bringing his torso to hers. "Clothing. Off." She demanded. "Want to see what I've got."

He laughed, a low rumbling noise. "So much for letting me to be in control." But his laughter was pleased, inviting her to join in. "I need my legs free," he told her, and she released him immediately. He shucked his pants off with one hand, never letting her wrists go.

"Commando?" She was amused, her voice low and surprisingly seductive. She didn't recognize herself.

"I was out of underwear," he said, blushing just a little. "It's drying in my shower."

Lily felt something twist inside her, a few inches below her heart and above her gut. It hurt, but like a limb snapping back into place; a hurt followed by a sense of rightness, of something broken suddenly fixed.

Fuck me, she was going to say, had intended to say: trying to keep the encounter hard and fun and without any kind of commitment implied or asked for.

"Make love to me," she said instead, sitting up enough to whisper the demand in his ear, making sure that her tongue touched the outer tip of that ear.

"Oh, Lily, don't tempt me so…."

His mouth abandoned her breast and moved lower, sliding over her belly until she giggled because it tickled. His tongue dipped into her belly button, circled around it, then moved lower.

"Hang on a second, I've got this," he said when he reached the waistband of her pants. She waited, and then started to laugh as his teeth closed on the snap of her slacks. Her laughter stopped the moment he had them down on her hips, and his mouth went directly for the damp cotton of her panties.

"Jesus, Lily…I'm so going to make you come for me…"

Then her panties were shoved down her legs, and his mouth was on her. Both of his hands were on her thighs now, holding her open, but Lily felt no desire to move her arms from where he had pinned her. His tongue slid inside her, and lapped like he was the kitten and she was a deep, deep dish of cream.

"Oh…" Lily caught the endearment before it fell off her own tongue, biting her lip as Jon made her hips buck upward. She had asked him to make love to her and that was exactly what he was doing. But it wasn't enough. She needed more.

Her exercise routine might not have given her a flat

stomach, but there were muscles underneath the rounding, and she was able to sit up without using her legs, catching Jon unawares. A push back, and he was the one at her mercy, her legs straddling his hips as they sprawled on the floor, her hands on his shoulders, pressing him down.

"Wanna play rough, do you?" he asked, recovering quickly. His eyes were as hotly focused as ever, even as the muscles in his face were loose and soft, and she couldn't resist kissing the tip of his nose, watching with delight as his eyes almost crossed, trying to follow her.

"Want you," she told him. "In me. Now." She grinned, fierce to match his stare. "We can play…later."

Later. There would be a later. He took that promise and ran with it, fastening his mouth to hers in a deep sweet kiss, even as his hands brought her down onto his cock, sliding into her wet folds like coming home, like some impossible perfect fit. She wasn't warm, she was hot, and tight, and a little voice in his head warned him that they weren't using protection even as she shifted on him and he groaned into her mouth.

They fought for the lead, first one and then the other setting the pace. Sweat glistened and thoughts fled, until Lily arched her back and lifted her face, tears streaming.

"Lily?"

"Don't…keep going, keep…"

Her fingers gripped his shoulders, and she tucked her chin forward, hair falling around her face as she looked down into his eyes. It was almost a challenge, that wet stare, and he met it, keeping eye contact even as his own orgasm built.

She blinked first, her eyes closing, that odd shadow closing half a second before her outer lid, but then she was falling into a silky black spiral, totally caught up in her own sensations. She collapsed in his arms for a second time that night, his fingers tightening on her arms as he pulled out, reaching his own apex against the pale, sleek skin of her thigh. She swore, and he laughed, and followed her over into exhaustion.

He woke up, immediately aware he wasn't at home, or in the usual scratchy-sheeted hotel room. These sheets were soft, almost silky, as was the body snuggled next to him. They had made their way to the bed at some point during the evening, holding hands and stumbling against things in the dark.

He ran his finger along the lines of one creamy-skinned shoulder, listening to the sound of her breathing. Lily kept the thermostat in her condo higher than he was used to. Post-sex sweat always seemed, well, sweatier than when he worked out in the gym. Probably because you didn't usually end up cuddled with your workout partner.

The thought made Patrick snort with horrified laughter—his usual workout partner, Cal, was not exactly cuddling material, being six foot three and three feet wide, all of it muscle. Attractive to some, he supposed, but…

Yes, he definitely preferred them pocket-size and curvy. Call him old-fashioned.

His Venus rolled over to face the sound, opened one eye, then the other.

"Mornin'?" It sounded as though she was begging for a negative answer.

"Not quite yet," he reassured her. "But I should…"

"Yeah."

The dialogue sounded awkward. But he couldn't quite stop smiling, and Lily raised herself up so that she rested on one elbow, her dark curls falling over one bare shoulder like some not-quite soft-core-movie poster. Her skin was flushed across her chest and neck, and there was a dark purple hickey forming just below her jawline.

He didn't remember doing that, but the evidence was, well, evident.

"I have to go. Boss wants a status report, and I have to check the overnights, and…"

He didn't want to go anywhere. He wanted to stay, and not just because he was worried about that freak finding her. He wanted to stay in that bed, the sheets smelling of them, and feel her legs tangled in his, her hair tickling under his nose. He wanted to be able to roll over and have her in his arms, ready and warm and willing. Or even just sleeping: anticipation, when you knew what was waiting for you, was sugar-sweet.

She blinked lazily, and he was reminded again of the strangeness of the night before. But she seemed to have forgotten it somehow. Or dispensed with it as not important. Either way, he hesitated to bring it up again. Not here. Not now. Stress. She was under a lot of stress. Bad dreams and dizziness—she hadn't had dinner last night, either.

"I'll be fine. And I won't be offended by your early-morning departure. Go."

"I'll call you." He was still worried. That was a surprise, and an unwelcome one. Worry was personal. He couldn't afford that personal twitch, couldn't be distracted by it. Not now. Not yet. He hadn't thought about that when he had daydreamed his seduction of the delectable, desirable Lily. Idiot.

"Mmm." She smiled at him and he lost track of his thoughts again. "You'd better. You need coffee?"

"I'll get some on my way. Go back to sleep."

He kissed her on the tip of her nose, and she scrunched it under his touch, then sank down into the blankets and sighed, sliding back into sleep even as he picked up his clothes and headed for the bathroom. He should have already been focusing on the case, on what might be waiting for him, but all he could do was keep thinking that Lily Malkin was...

Was more than he had been expecting. Far, far more.

Chapter 10

Dale Mortman, agent in charge of the D.C. CID and various other governmental initials, was a very patient man. But even patience could reach an end, and his voice at the other end of the standard-issue police department phone carried that warning. "You realize what you're asking?"

Patrick crossed his legs more comfortably under the desk, stretched out in his borrowed chair and rolled his eyes to the heavens as though to ask for patience. "I'm not twelve. Yes, I know what I'm asking. Look, right now this is a mild curiosity that could become a localized media circus. Fine, not our problem, locals can handle it, yeah, I know. But his words are…worrying me."

The cat woman. She knows. The recording Petrosian

had gotten of the phone call replayed in his head on a seemingly endless loop.

What did Lily know? Did she even know that she knew? Or was it all part of this guy—the Night Serpent's—game, or psychosis, or whatever?

That was Patrick's job: to find out. It was what he was good at. All he had to do was step back and look at the pieces. And not think about how one of those pieces was probably just waking up right now, heading into the shower, standing under a stream of hot water, lathering up her breasts….

Yeah, definitely not thinking about that.

"We are not unaffected by the thought of a threat to a civilian…."

Patrick took another sip of his coffee and made a face. He should have accepted Lily's offer—this stuff was worse than swill. At least in the good old days you could count on one cop per shift knowing how to make a decent pot. Now, with the "pod" machines, it was all mechanized, and—in his opinion—crap.

"Save me the canned PR bullshit," he told his boss. "Just tell me I'm a good boy and to get on with my job."

Dale had a sigh you could hear from one end of the Beltway to the other, and no hesitation about letting loose with it.

"If you think you have a handle on this guy… Run with it. Whatever you need by way of support, CID will do their best to supply. Just try not to need anything expensive that I'll have to explain at a budget meeting, okay? And I need you back here by next Tuesday."

"Got it. Thanks."

It wasn't a home run—he'd *wanted* to get Lily some protection, above and beyond the little that the local cops could provide, but without an actual threat from a certified serial killer, he'd known better than to even ask. His personal involvement might be clouding his judgment, but it wasn't making him an idiot.

At least now he knew that his requests for information would get priority, without having to go the favor-for-a-friend route. Or getting Lily involved any further.

The bustle around him parted for a moment, and the smell of stale smoke and old coffee swirled down to him. Petrosian, scratchy-voiced, like a guy who had been chain-smoking all shift.

"You hear what they're calling him?"

Patrick wondered where Petrosian smoked, since the entire precinct was now officially and legally smoke free, all the way out to the parking lot. "The Night Serpent. Yeah." The morning news had picked up the story, lacking anything more bloodthirsty coming in overnight. He had heard a squib on the cab's radio, on his way. Inevitable, considering the guy's comments. More evocative than "sick bastard," he supposed. Sold more papers, got better ratings.

"It mean anything?" Petrosian pulled a chair from behind the other desk and sat down in it. "Give you a clue into his alleged mind?"

"Maybe." His brain went into "sift and filter" mode. "Serpents and cats are, historically and allegorically, enemies. They're also, however, both aligned with the devil in Christian mythology. Our unsub is killing cats in a ritualistic manner, and then displaying them in a circle, nose to tail. Similar to that of a snake, in both Celtic and Norse mythologies. I've got a search running to see if there's been anything entered into the system similar in the past twenty years." Lily hadn't found anything, but his search engine had access to more data. "Based on the witness's description, this guy's not old enough to have done anything noteworthy before then, or if he did, it would be under juvie seal."

"In other words, you got shit."

"I have…a couple of theories. None of which get us anywhere. That the tox report?"

Petrosian handed it to him. "Yeah. Same as the others—clean as a cat's innards can be. This guy is doing it all by hand. You ever get around to asking Lily about your idea, that he's another cat-whisperer type?"

The question was casual, but the glance sent along with it wasn't. Patrick suddenly felt like he was fourteen years old and caught trying to feel up Judy Clare after gym class. He shook his head. "No. She was still pretty shook up…. You think you could talk her into going to see a doctor?" He carefully didn't specify what sort of doctor; he honestly wasn't sure. She was exhibiting signs that in another person he would consider warnings of a breakdown, if not an actual psychotic break. And yet, having looked into her eyes, felt her in his arms—even against all evidence, he didn't believe that she was crazy.

He didn't know *what* to believe.

Petrosian slouched farther into his chair. "I'm not her daddy, Patrick. She's a grown woman, she does what she wants." And *with whom* was loudly unspoken.

The personal undercurrents thus navigated to their satisfaction, both men relaxed slightly and returned to the case.

He had not slept well since he saw the woman. That golden glow inside her haunted him, distracted him. And finally, finally, he understood the message that had been sent, in her appearance. A gift from Herself; one of her Handmaidens, yes, but innocent in this world. Born fresh, clean. Ready for him to write his message on.

He was smart. Had always been smart. Smarter than his teachers ever knew. Smart like…like the serpent coiled in the grass. The Night Serpent, they were calling him now. He liked that, yes. The serpent was wise. Don't show yourself. Don't waste energy attacking everything that moves. Let others flush out your target, and then strike once, effectively.

His knife to the beasts' throats; like a cobra's strike: swift and certain.

It was not cruelty, it was not bloodlust; it was not any of those things the reporters were claiming on television. It was need.

That last time he had felt it; as the blood dripped into the circle, he had felt the earth shift, the gates begin to open. He was almost there, the time was almost right, the cats were almost right…but something essential wasn't present. She wasn't appeased. Wasn't satisfied by his offerings, his sacrifice.

But he had another chance. One more before the window closed, his third chance was up, and he was trapped in this hell for another lifetime. She had given him that; had shown him the cat woman, the one who glimmered with gold, who brought the beasts to hand. She was the key to the lock. She would be able to tell him what he had been doing wrong.

And now he knew where she was. All he had to do was collect her.

Lily woke at nine that morning, sat up in panic before remembering that she was off today, and then fell back onto the bed, only to be reminded by the not-unpleasant aches that she had not spent the night alone. Or sleeping.

Oh God. She had actually…they had actually…

Not that she regretted it, she thought. She just wished it had been under less…weird circumstances. The night before was sort of fuzzy, after they told her about the phone call, and her inclusion in it, but she remembered getting dizzy, and Jon's arms around her, and…

And the memories that followed *that* made a flush rise up her cheeks. Aches in her thighs, oh yes. And also her shoulders, and her arms, and her stomach…

He was gone, long gone if the temperature of the pillow next to her was any indication. She had some memory of that as well, of waking and speaking and the faintest caress of his hand on her face before he left.

Getting out of bed, she ran through her normal routines before realizing, halfway through her shower, that she had nowhere to go and nothing to do today. She was supposed to work at the shelter this afternoon; they were gearing up for the year-end donation appeal, and she was supposed to do her share of envelope stuffing and stamping. But she had agreed to stay away from the shelter for a few days, she did remember that.

"I suppose I could get someone to bring over a box or two of letters," she told herself. Even Special Agent Jon T. Patrick couldn't object to that, and she'd love to see some overeager reporter try to stick a microphone in Ronnie's face. They'd end up tasting it all the way down their throat, if the shelter director was feeling particularly cranky. Or she would use the opportunity to get some free media attention for the shelter. Either way, goodness.

Amused despite the situation, Lily got out of the shower, grabbed the thick black towel off the rack and dried herself off. Clad in a soft robe, she padded to the kitchen to make herself some coffee and see what was up with the world.

The talking heads were still doing their shtick, but if the bastard who was killing cats was still newsworthy, it had been featured before she tuned in.

She would give this house arrest two days. Then she was supposed to be back on shift at the bank, and she would, by God be there.

The phone rang, and she jumped, then, shaking her head at the sudden attack of nerves, crossed the room and picked up the receiver.

"Yes?"

"Heya."

She suddenly felt like a teenager with her first crush, curling the phone cord around her fingers and leaning against the wall, the phone pressed to her ear.

"Hey yourself."

"I figured you'd be up by now. You okay?"

"I'm…okay, yeah."

What did you say to the man you'd met only days before? The man who had left your bed before dawn? The man you knew better than to get involved with, and still did?

"I'm not very good at this." She had always been brutally honest. No reason to stop now.

"I think you underestimate yourself," he said, and she flushed again.

"I mean…"

"I know what you mean. Don't worry, Lily. I think you're amazing, and brave, and a lot of other things I'm not going to say out loud with half a dozen cops sitting in the same room with me pretending that they're not listening in."

She was *definitely* blushing, now.

"I just wanted to check in, see… You okay?" he repeated.

She was puzzled—what did he think would be wrong?—when she remembered. Being cold. Not just dizzy, but dislocated. Hearing voices.

Mother, forgive me!

"Lily?"

"I'm here. I'm…okay."

No, she wasn't. She suddenly felt ill. Her stomach hurt, as if she'd been throwing up, and the muscles in her neck and shoulders hurt in a bad way, not the good of before, and her eyes were red and dry like they'd been sandblasted. Like she had the flu, or something.

"I'm okay," she said again. "Jon, I've got to go. I'll talk to you later, all right?"

She hung up the phone and made it to the bathroom just in time to dry heave into the toilet. She was shivering and weak kneed, but her head stayed clear, and her memories were her own.

Maybe she *was* coming down with the flu.

She called the shelter after that, planning to give some excuse, but none was needed. They had seen the news reports as well, and put two and two together and come up with five reasons why she should not come in that day, even before she announced her intention to take a few days off.

"Girl, that may be the most sensible thing I've ever heard you say, and you were *born* sensible," Ronnie cackled over the phone. "Stay home. Stay out of sight. And if anyone comes here looking for you, we'll sit on him until your gorgeous Fibbie comes to arrest him."

"He's not my Fibbie," Lily protested, but could feel herself flushing again as she said it. Maybe not hers, exactly, but she had laid a claim…and so had he. She touched the bruise on her neck and was suddenly almost thankful for the excuse not to have to explain it to anyone. Although if it weren't for this loon, she would never have met Jon, so there wouldn't be anything to explain….

She hung up the phone and reached for the cleaning supplies. Anything to keep from thinking. Not about this Night Serpent and whatever he was planning, not about Agent Patrick and his disturbing ability to get inside all of her defenses, and absolutely not about the weird dreams and weirder dizziness she had been feeling.

Although she hadn't had any dreams last night. And she felt fine this morning, until Jon's call. No weirdness with her eyes, no dizziness, no strange smells or sounds…

So maybe all you needed was a good romp between the sheets? It was a lowering thought, but the medicine had been sweet, so she really couldn't complain.

The day went faster than she expected; she finally got the deep cleaning of the kitchen done, and all of the laundry, and she was contemplating actually washing the floor, when the boxes arrived from the shelter. A hundred letters in one, a hundred envelopes in the other, with a huge roll of labels and stamps to go with it.

"You did ask," Nancy said half apologetically, handing the boxes over. Lily looked cautiously over the other woman's shoulder, but didn't see any news vans or stray reporters lurking.

"Thanks. You want some coffee, or…?"

"Nah, I gotta get back. And…Lil?"

"Yes?"

"Be careful, okay? Some woman came around the shelter this morning asking about you, and we've had a couple of phone calls. Reporters. Ronnie didn't want to say anything, didn't want you to worry, but…it's only fair you know, I thought. We didn't tell them anything, of course. Just that you were a volunteer and we didn't give out names, and certainly not addresses, but…"

"I'm careful," Lily assured her. "And the police are

doing regular drive-bys." An Officer Stephens was on the day shift, with his partner whose name she hadn't gotten, a dark-skinned, annoyed-looking woman. She hadn't met the night shift, but she knew they were out there. "If anyone tries to stick a camera in my window, I'll flash 'em."

Nancy laughed and left, reassured. Lily took the boxes back into the dining room and set them on the table. Some more coffee, and she should be able to get through this before it was time to make dinner.

She carefully did not let herself wonder if Jon would show up for that meal.

Chapter 11

Agent Patrick ducked into the darkened room, barely the size of a supply closet, and shut the door behind him. "What've we got?"

The room was filled with monitors; on two of them, tapes were running, the familiar black-and-white flicker of security tapes, the time and date running at the bottom right hand of the screen.

"Security-cam footage. Came in this afternoon." Petrosian tapped one of the technicians on the shoulder. "Run it again."

The tape flickered, blurred in rewind, and then started again from the beginning. Two views, one on each screen.

"These are from our local zoo," Petrosian said. "Not going to compete with the big'uns, but it has a few decent exhibits. Out in Dover, about ten-minute drive north of here. Our guy has a car."

"You sure it's him?"

The first tape showed a sweep of the exterior, one side of a low-slung building gray and black in the predawn light. "The monkey house," Petrosian identified it. "If that is our guy, he did not do his homework."

A shadow flitted across the tapes. Tall, fast-moving and agile. No way to identify it, even with well-placed house lights. The camera clearly caught him jimmying the window, however.

"Silent alarm," one of the techs said. "Alerts the owners and the security company without freaking out the critters."

"Or letting the intruder know he's been twigged." Scaring someone away before they even got in was better security, but if an intruder was determined, he wouldn't be scared off by anything short of a shotgun being loaded behind his ear.

The second tape started rolling. This was inside a long open space filled with dead trees and what looked like—Patrick squinted—yes, old tire swings. What looked like a shallow pond lay at the far end of the space.

"Tiger enclosure. Damn, he's got balls. No way I'd go anywhere near there, not without a stun gun and backup." The second tech shook his head, either in shock or admiration.

At night, the cats were kept in a separate enclosure, but the intruder didn't seem to realize that, looking into the wooden structures as though expecting to find a cat hidden there.

"This guy may have done some research, but yeah, he's not all that clued in, otherwise he wouldn't be wasting his time there. And what does he think he's going to do when he finds them, anyway?"

"He's not a pro," Petrosian said. "Like a junkie tossing a house for whatever he can pawn fast, he's going by gut and instinct. Here's where it gets interesting."

The intruder lifted his head, as though hearing a noise, then turned and headed for a small door at the end of the enclosure. The tape stuttered, and then jump-cut to another location, this one an indoor hallway lit by fluorescent bulbs, with a handful of doors off to the left-hand side. The intruder walked quickly along, stopping at the second door as though pulled by a magnet.

"That's where the younger cats are kept," Petrosian told Patrick.

The guy knew. Not because he'd looked at plans beforehand, or read a sign on the door; he *knew*. Just the way Patrick knew the guy knew: not brain-knowing, but gut-knowing. Spooky-knowing.

The intruder had just placed his hand on the doorknob when the door at the end of the hallway burst open, the lights flashed on, and two—no, three security guards came into the hall.

Patrick noted absently that they had pretty good form, for rental cops. They didn't do anything wrong. It wasn't the fault of their training, what happened next.

"Stop where you are!" the lead guard shouted, going low so his companions would have a clear shot over his head if the intruder decided to get cute.

The unsub turned, his hand falling away from the

doorknob, raising his hands as though to indicate surrender. The camera wasn't advanced enough to zoom in on his face, but Patrick was pretty sure it creased up as though he'd tasted something sour, and then he started yelling. It was gibberish, nonsense words, but in a pattern that sounded as if he was saying something with meaning. Patrick frowned. It sounded…like the words that Lily had said last night. Or not the exact words, but in the same language.

Connection. But what kind, and what did it mean? And was Lily keeping something from him? He hoped not. He really, really hoped not, and not only because it would make him seven different kinds of fool. "Do we have any idea what he's saying?"

"Not a clue. Was hoping your boys would be able to do something about that."

Patrick nodded; he had been about to request a copy of the tapes for exactly that reason. "Give me a copy, and an audio strip-out. I'll see what they come back with."

"Already on digital. Give me an e-mail address and I can zip 'em over posthaste."

Some days Patrick really loved technology.

"Hang on," Petrosian warned. "There's more."

The unsub's left hand lowered, still over his shoulder and not looking as if it was reaching for anything, but suddenly there was a small object in his hand, about the size and width of a CD. He shook it at the guards as though expecting something to happen. When it didn't, he let out a roar and rushed them, knocking the first one over and colliding with two and three. There was a strange spray of sparks where their bodies met, and then the guards fell to the floor, gasping and grabbing at their clothing, trying to put out the flames that had somehow started in the fabric.

The intruder threw his head back and yowled something, waving the object at the ceiling, and then ran out the door.

The tape ended.

"What the hell?" Patrick asked, not expecting an answer.

"Some kind of flamethrower, we guess. Butane torch, like they use in kitchens?"

Patrick had used a kitchen torch before, in a miserable attempt to make crème brûlée. They didn't look anything like that, nor did they throw sparks without visible flames, even when they malfunctioned.

"Anyway, the guards are okay. But before the guy ran, he opened half a dozen cages. Hell, he stopped to do it, even with the alarms wailing. Freaked-out critters everywhere. Zoo staff is trying to round them up, and keep the predators from eating the other displays."

"Nice." Patrick's tone indicated he thought that it was anything but.

"That guy's nuts," the tech who had earlier commented on his cojones said, this time far less admiringly. Nobody in the room disagreed.

A few hours later, Patrick wandered out of the building to get some fresh air and clear his head. Something about what he'd seen was bothering him, but he couldn't quite place what. Other than the fact that the unsub might have been speaking the same unknown language that Lily—a potential target of obsession of the killer—had muttered in during her dizzy spell. A dizzy spell that also included physical symptoms that were weird at best, and worrisome at most.

All the pieces were important, Patrick was sure of it. Lily's connection to cats, the Night Serpent's need to kill them, the shared language, the physical symptoms…

He just had no damn idea what any one of them meant, much less how they fit together.

"Hey." Petrosian, cigarette dangling from his lips, unlit.

"Those things are gonna kill you," Patrick said, indicating it with a jerk of his chin.

"Only if I'm lucky," Petrosian replied, the inevitable cop response. "Besides, bastards won't even let me light up anymore."

He was going to make a wiseass comeback, but his phone vibrated, demanding his attention. "Patrick."

He shifted his cell phone to the other ear to hear better. "Uh-huh. Great. What've you got for me?" The worst part of the job was waiting for other people to do their job. The best part was when they came through, setting you on the next stage of investigation. That was when the blood surged, the brain leaped into overdrive, the neurons all fired and the case got solved.

"It was what?"

The voice of the FBI linguist came through the phone lines, clear, sarcastic and heavily put upon. "Ancient Egyptian, New Kingdom, around 1500 B.C. Do you know how long it took us to figure that out and

find someone who could translate? This ain't Stargate.
We don't have that kind of brainpower just sitting
around twiddling their thumbs."

"But you guys are brilliant and figure it out anyway."

"No, we know enough to call the Smithsonian. And
even they aren't sure they've got it right." The linguist
rustled paper for effect, then read off the translation
for the agent.

"Jesus. You're sure?"

"Hell, no, we're not sure. But that's out best guess.
It make any sense to you?"

Yes. Yes, it did. And it made his blood run cold.

*The Way Must be Opened. Her Blood will Turn the
Key.*

"Pack something. Basics, jeans and sweaters. Toiletries."

"What?" Lily stepped back to let Jon in, surprised
to see two uniformed officers come in right on his heels.
One of them was Stephens, of her daytime drive-by
patrol. She knew him vaguely from previous cat-related
cases. She gave him a small wave, and he shuffled his
feet, clearly awkward with actually being in her home.
The other was a man she didn't know, who was carefully not looking at her.

"You can't stay here. He hurt people last night, Lily.
Whatever he was before, he's escalated. And he's got
you in his brain. I want you somewhere else, now."

"You want?" Lily stood in front of him, her hands
on her hips. The solid build she had admired—
caressed—the night before was now a barrier, a chal-

lenge to her. "What about what I want?" Her eyes widened, and she felt her fingers flex in sudden agitation. How dare he just drop this on her, as if it was all his decision and she had no say in anything at all. When did she become his property, just because they'd slept together?

"Lily, please." There were two cops with him. Would they side with her, or him? Jon—Agent Patrick—would rather they were federal agents, men he could boss around rather than play nicely with.

She tried to rein in her anger. He probably had his reasons, she was sure he had his reasons. Pure logic said that if she was at real risk, he could protect her better somewhere else, somewhere he could control everything, someplace secret. Wasn't that the point of safe houses, in every TV show she'd ever seen?

Logic, though, seemed to have gone out the door the same time he came in and started ordering her around all the wrong way, and she couldn't seem to stop herself from reacting badly.

She was angry. No, she was furious. She was also, she discovered, more than a little turned on by the stubborn set of his jaw, and the way his eyes had gone flat not in anger, but determination. Lily was taken aback by that realization. She didn't like men who were bossy, any more than she liked ones who were overly ambitious. But this was…it was the whole FBI-man thing. Power. Not ambition, which had made her uneasy, but a man aware of his own abilities and consequence, and not unwilling to use them.

She reacted to it, yeah, okay. Male-in-Authority

kink, check. But getting told what to do and don't ask questions? Her spine stiffened like a steel rod in reaction against it. She was an adult, damn it. She had her own power, in her own right, and she would not let him ride roughshod over it. And if that made her unreasonable so be it. She was tired of *men* always deciding her fate.

"No." She shook her head, glaring at him. "This is my home. I'm as safe here as I will be anywhere, and a lot more comfortable. You have no idea that he's actually going to threaten me, you said so yourself. He thinks I know something, something that he needs. That doesn't sound like intent to commit violence. And even if he does come here, I have my security system, I have you, and now I've got two cops of my very own." She assumed that they were here to protect her, and not just carry her suitcase to the car, anyway.

"Damn it, Lily, it will be easier to protect you in a safe house." He ran a hand through his hair and stared at something over her shoulder.

"You don't own me," she said. "And you don't get to order me around." His gaze swung back to her and she was struck again by the intensity of his stare. Burning, focused and more than a little unnerving. The man who had made love to her was gone, and the man who tracked killers for a living was back.

"It's important for you to maintain control, isn't it?" he asked, obviously trying to be reasonable.

"Don't try to analyze me," she snapped. "I pay someone to do that. And years of therapy have told me that yes, I need control. I need to be the only one who makes decisions for me. If you have a problem with that—"

He grabbed her arm and tugged her off to the side, away from the overtly eavesdropping cops. "I'm not going caveman on you," he said. "I'm just trying to do my job. Lily. It's only for a little while. Just to be safe."

She stared at him, then back at the cops. There was something he wasn't telling her, and that cooled her anger even as determination solidified. "I can't do this. I can't… Post guards at my doors and windows if you want. But I'm not going anywhere."

She didn't know why she was being so stubborn. But it felt right. This was her home, a place she had worked hard to afford, to make into a refuge, a place where she felt comfortable in a world that she never quite felt in sync with.

Now he wanted to take her away from it, in the name of "safety." Without telling her why. Even she knew that if there was no safety here, there wasn't safety anywhere. No matter how safe a safe house might be. The Night Serpent wanted her, he would find her. It was that simple.

The phone rang, and she broke away from him to answer it.

"Who is this?" She looked at Jon, who had followed her into the kitchen.

"You know." The voice was flat, but somehow wired, as though it were about to explode. It made her skin crawl just hearing it.

"I don't know."

"Yes. You do. He's there, so you know what's happening. You can fix it, I know you can. She told me. She showed me. You're the key. You're the messenger. You have to tell me what I'm doing wrong. How do I convince Her to open the door? You *know!*"

Seeing her agitation, Jon took the phone from her. "This is Special Agent Patrick. Who am I speaking with?"

There was silence. "The Night Serpent. But you knew that already. Let me talk to the woman. I don't want to talk to you."

The smart thing to do would be to keep him on the phone, keep him talking. But there was no way to track him—with all the fuss over federal phone tapping recently, he hadn't wanted to open that can of worms to hook her phone up, hadn't thought the guy would contact her like this. Lily was right; he had been so focused on the physical risk, he had overlooked the more passive threat, the indirect approach....

The Way Must be Opened. Her Blood will Turn the Key.

"The lady doesn't want to talk to you. What makes you think she'd talk to a cat killer like you, anyway?"

The Serpent took a deep breath, as though the accusation had shocked him. "We do things…that must be done. There is always a price. She understood. She showed me the way, through Her beasts. But I can't open the door all the way. Let me talk to the woman, she's here to show me how!"

The Serpent's voice was rising, almost a yowl, and Patrick made the instinctive decision to hang up before the guy got even more worked up.

The moment the receiver was back in the cradle, he

punched in *57. Somewhere in the phone company's system, the caller's number, and Lily's number, were being recorded. Normally it took two or three calls to get the cops to do anything. Patrick suspected that he would be able to get a warrant for that number on just the one call.

"He knows my number."

"You're listed."

"I never thought… How did he learn my name?"

He wanted to take her in his arms, reassure her that nothing was wrong, everything was going to be okay. "Media, probably. Someone didn't see the harm in giving him the name of the cat lady the cops turn to. This guy, he looks normal. Sounds normal, if a little tightly wound. And you're a local celebrity…."

"Am not."

"You've been on TV, however unwillingly. To some people—" He broke off what he was saying and opened his cell phone, speed-dialing somewhere.

"It's Agent Patrick. The unsub just called the home of one of my consultants, made vaguely threatening comments. I've instituted a trace-back through the phone company. Yeah." He gave her phone number to whoever was on the other end of the line. "Yeah, thanks. I figured. No, I have officers here with me now, I'll arrange for them to…yeah. All right. Thanks."

"You'll arrange for them to do what?"

He didn't answer her, instead going back out to the foyer where the two uniforms were still standing, awkward without anything to do. He spoke to them softly, and she could see their entire demeanor change, going from useless to directed with the speed of a few words. He might have been an outsider, cops versus fed, but he was Authority.

Stephens looked over at her, and she shrugged, a sort of "you think I get any say in this?" motion. He gave a twisted smile in response that, weirdly, reassured her immensely. He wouldn't do anything that she didn't agree to.

"Lily, this is Officer Dunkirk—" that was the shorter one "—and this is—"

"Karl Stephens. We've met."

Stephens smiled at her again. "Ma'am."

She nodded her head politely at them both. "You're going to be my guard dogs, is that it?"

"Ma'am. We're good at barking. And completely yard trained."

Stephens clearly had the right attitude about all of this.

"All right, I'll keep them. But only if it stays low key. I don't want any of my neighbors upset, or the condo board screaming about loitering strangers and 'bad elements' hanging around the building."

Stephens didn't seem to mind being called a bad element, either. "If anyone asks, ma'am, we'll tell them we're part of the mayor's initiative to get more patrols actually out on the street, meeting locals and getting our faces known."

"Great. You mean I'll have to vote for him next election?"

The laughter didn't quite overcome the irritation she was feeling, though. When Jon turned to her as though to continue their discussion, she felt the urge again to hiss at him, warning him away. It was all…too fast. Too much. He came in here as though he had the right to reorder her life, tell her where to go and what to do. Arrange for cops to guard her, as though she were some sort of possession…

A small part of her mind knew that her reaction was overblown, that he wasn't thinking that—probably, that she was reacting to things that weren't in the picture. And Aggie had arranged for the cops in the first place— Aggie had been the one to suggest her staying home, playing it safe. But she felt as though it was *Jon* who was steamrolling over her, refusing to accept her ability to make decisions, to control her own life.

And yet she reacted positively when he went all alpha male on her. She admired his competence, his aggression. She found it appealing, sexy.

And she…feared him for it at the same time.

It didn't make any sense. But it was real, and Lily had learned that while facing your fears was good, denying that they were real was the worst thing she could possibly do.

She needed space to figure this out. Space she wasn't going to get with Alpha Male Special Agent Jon T. Patrick trying to protect her.

"I've already allowed enough changes, against a threat you aren't even sure exists. No more." She stared at him, daring him to override her. "I stay here. They can stay. You have to go."

It was cold, standing in the shadow of the old tree, but for once he did not mind it. The cold was nothing compared to the anticipation inside. So close. So very, very close…and so easy to find her, after all! To hear her voice…

It was a small, narrow building, two stories, crowded on either side by identical structures. A one-car garage shared a driveway with the building next door. The symmetry of the structures pleased him.

Lights were on in the lower level of the house, and people moved in front of the windows. One figure, slender and short, then another, taller and bulkier. A man. The Night Serpent scowled. Who was that man with her?

A sound; the front door opening, shadows under the lights. The man was leaving. Good. And two more, behind him—were they guards? Attendants? There, they were leaving as well. The man drove away, the others walked down the street, the slow pace of trained fighters. Guards, but not belonging to the man? No matter. They were no longer in the house. They had left her to him.

And yet, the thought that she was now left alone disturbed him. She too should have attendants about her, attendants and guards to protect her, protect that brightness within her. It was wrong, as wrong as everything else in this world. The way he had seen her before, that was right. That was correct. She should be striding free, not locked away in that narrow house. There was so much inside her, so much glinting gold, this world could not, *would* not reward, any more than it rewarded his own superiority.

But he knew her value. He would reward her once

he got what he needed from her. But first, the woman must tell him what he needed to know.

He needed to talk to her again. Now that the man and the guards were out of the way.

He stepped out of the shelter of the tree, and then stopped. One of the guards was back, a rucksack over his shoulder. He went up the stairs, and she let him in without hesitation.

"Damn." The Night Serpent glared, but the door remained closed. After a while, a light went on upstairs, while one remained on in the first level.

They were in for the night.

He hesitated, wanting to stay, watch over the house in hopes of a chance to speak with the woman alone. But the beasts needed feeding and watering; it would not be good for them to become angry before he could ask them to intercede for him. No, it would not do at all.

Chapter 12

Lily was fuming. She had thought it was all settled. She had been a good girl, allowed Stephens and Dunkirk to babysit her all weekend without complaint, alternating shifts sleeping on her sofa. She had taken her leave from the shelter. She had even rescheduled her hairstylist appointment, leaving her with a mass of unruly curls that she had resorted to stuffing under a baseball cap rather than fight with Jon about going out in public spaces. But this was… This was one step beyond too much.

"I don't need an escort," she snarled.

"Fine." Cool, oh so cool, Agent Patrick was. Like nothing could scratch his surface.

She glared at him. He ignored her, pulling the car out of the parking lot. It was his rental, an economy compact, and handled like crap. She missed her own car. She missed driving herself. She had been fuming about it all day, even as she was smilingly pleasant to the customers.

"You are the most high-handed, overbearing, impossible, *insane* human being—"

"I told you—you're not going anywhere alone."

"I didn't need a driver. I don't need a guard. Bad enough you and Aggie have the boys wandering around my house...."

"*The boys,* is it?" She thought she heard jealousy in his voice, but decided that she was probably imagining things. "Lily, we don't have patrols assigned to your home on a whim."

"No, just a theory," she muttered, and was almost immediately ashamed of herself. It was a theory she agreed with, even if she didn't like the results.

He ignored her, and went on. "That bastard is still on the loose. He knows where you live, your name, he probably knows where you work by now, if he didn't before—you really want to give him a clear chance at you? Would you rather have a patrol car drive you everywhere?"

"I want to go to the shelter."

It was a ninety-degree turn in the conversation, but it made perfect sense to Lily. She had been away for over a week now, thanks to Patrick and Aggie's insistence, and she missed her cats. Ronnie had been updating her by e-mail on who was adopted, and what new cats had come in, but it wasn't the same. They needed her there. More, she needed to be there.

"Lily, you know why…."

"Yes. I know why. And yes, I want to stay out of this guy's sights more than you can believe. That's the only reason you've won chauffeur's rights. But I can't…"

She paused, and then decided to fight dirty.

"You don't understand. I was seven the first time it hit. This total, unrelenting, impossible-to-describe feeling." Even now, talking about it, she felt cold, even with the heat on in the car. "It wasn't fear, or discomfort, or the usual sort of phobic terror. Just…every inch of my body felt uneasy. Something was wrong, and something was coming at me, and I had no way to deal with it because I didn't even know what it was. I couldn't explain it to my parents. But I knew what triggered it."

Patrick made a sound that she took to mean "go on."

"Cats. They would walk into a room and stop and…*look* at me. That old saying, 'A cat may look at a king'? It doesn't mean what you think it means. It's not about a cat's rights…it's about their abilities. Their…. A cat looks at a king, and he doesn't see a member of royalty. He sees a human, in all its vain ego and uselessness."

She paused, feeling her mouth dry up in a way it hadn't for years. She swallowed anyway, and went on.

"A cat looks at you that way, and they see all the way through you. At first I thought that they were… that they didn't like me. But they kept coming to me after they looked at me like that. They would rub against me, and demand to be picked up and carried, and I *couldn't*. I couldn't hold them, touch them. After a while I couldn't even be near them. I couldn't bear to have them look at me. I used to cry the moment one of them came into the room. I wasn't allergic, I was *traumatized*."

"And now you work with them…?" He clearly didn't understand how that leap had happened, or why.

"I guess there's only so long you can let something like that rule your life. It took me a lot of therapy, a lot of talking myself up to it. I'm still not…entirely comfortable with cats outside the shelter, but when I'm here working with the kittens, or even the older cats, I can stand to have them look at me. It's okay. *I'm* okay."

She paused again.

"I need that right now. I need a sense of being okay. All right?"

There was a long silence from the driver's side, and even without looking she knew that she had him. What else could he do but give in?

"Okay. I'm going to regret this, but…okay." He turned the car into a strip-mall parking lot to turn around. The shelter was on the other side of town. "An hour, and you stay inside, and away from any visitors, and I'm with you at all times. All right?"

She smiled, just a little. "All right. Thank you."

The familiar facade of the shelter made a tightness she didn't even know was in her chest ease slightly. She walked through the door, Patrick a disapproving shadow on her heels, intending to go directly to the main office to say hello and let them know that she was there. But the moment she entered the lobby, the tight-ness in her chest came back like a metal fist squeezing tight, and she would have fallen to her knees if he hadn't been there to catch her.

"I'm making a habit of this," he said in her ear, the humor not masking his worry.

"Something's wrong. Something's…" She started to hyperventilate, each breath coming faster and faster until she felt as though she could never catch up with the air leaving her lungs. Weight crushed her rib cage, and sweat poured down her neck and the sides of her face. It was never like this, not even at its worst. This was…gods, the *anger* she felt! The outrage, and the snarling fear…

"Lily?" His voice was edging on panicked, and the fact of that gave her something to focus on. "Hey, anyone in there? I need some help!"

There was the rush of feet on the linoleum tile, and familiar hands on her. She should have been comforted, but instead she wanted to throw up.

Too much. Get them away from me. They'll see. They'll know. The guilt is all over me and I cannot bear it….

There was a howling in her ears, like a thousand sirens going off in a thunderstorm.

"Oh my God, what's going on?"

Lily came back to herself enough to realize, as some of the hands released her into a chair, that the howling came not from sirens but living throats. It was the full-bodied scream of an enraged cat. More than one, more than a dozen. It sounded as though every adult in the shelter was screaming at her.

Mother, I am sorry!

And then it stopped.

When Jon was able to focus again, he discovered that Lily had passed out in the chair.

"Damn it!" But even as he crouched over her and tried to remember what the protocol was for someone who had passed out, her eyes opened.

"Jesus."

He fell back onto his heels, staring. Her eyes—her lovely hazel eyes—had been completely swallowed up by pupil, until there was nothing left but inky blackness, looking back at him.

"Come on, Lily. Stay with me. How do you feel?" he said, touching her shoulder.

"I'm okay." She shook her head gently, as though testing her equilibrium. "I'm okay."

He would have argued that point, but his cell phone rang. Never taking his gaze off her, he answered. "Patrick. What? Are you sure? Where? I'll be right there."

He shut the phone with one hand, slipping it into his pocket while still keeping the other hand on Lily's shoulder.

"What is it?" Her voice was almost back to normal, but he didn't trust it. Not after the little scene he had just witnessed. And not the way her eyes still looked, all spooked and strange.

"Nothing. Just…you need to go…sit with the cats a little. They sounded as freaked as you looked."

"Jon. What?"

He looked into her weirdly black eyes, and was swallowed up by them.

"Jon?" Her voice dropped to a whisper, almost a purr. Soft. Seductive. "Tell me."

Sheer force of will brought him out of her eyes, allowing him to step back, literally and emotionally. *What the hell?*

But she was right; she deserved the truth. Even if he was going to have to sit on her afterward.

"That was Petrosian. Someone turned our unsub in, gave us a name. They want me down at the station, to go in after him."

"Let's go!" She struggled to get out of the chair, and he pushed her back down, gently. "Not you. Go get some cat therapy or have a cup of coffee or something."

"Patrick!" Her tone was outraged, and he couldn't help but smile. She was just adorable when she was pissed off, even more so than when she was trying to be a seductress. Seduction came naturally, in her every movement. He buried that thought, and tried to keep a stern face.

"Lily, you just had a major panic attack and collapsed. You're not going into a…" He looked at her, and lost track of his thoughts. Her eyes weren't back to normal yet, despite how she sounded and was acting. It was starting to really freak him out, all the more so because she seemed totally unaware of it.

"There might be cats there, Jon. Or… Whatever. You're going to need me. You do need me, otherwise you wouldn't have kept me around this long."

Damn it. Patrick wanted to send her home, if she wouldn't stay here. But she was right, if not for the reasons she thought. He stood and reached to give her a hand. "You'll stay in the car until the scene is cleared. And if you get dizzy, or anything—*anything*—gets weird, you tell me immediately. And the moment we're done, you're making an appointment with a doctor, because *something* is wrong. Deal?"

She grinned, triumphant. "Deal."

Chapter 13

He was restless, tired of waiting. Too many days of waiting, outside her home, outside her job. They never left her alone, and he did not want to approach her in front of others. She would hear him; they would not.

Now. Now, now now! His impatience practically danced on his shoulder.

Not yet.

But she's there. She's here. Right here.

And so is the man. And so are all those beasts. I will not go near that place; it stinks of Her. Now is not the right time. Not without proper preparation.

But she's never alone! Impatience wailed.

The voice was right; he could feel himself quiver with the need to reach her, talk to her. The cat woman. Time was short. Too short. He needed to know, *now*.

No more waiting. Everything was in place; all he needed was the woman.

If he could not go to her, then she would have to come to him.

They had gone directly from the shelter to the police station to meet with Petrosian, arguing all the while about what Lily called his overprotective machismo bullshit, and he called pragmatic protection of a material witness.

Lily didn't mince words. "I'm not a witness, material or otherwise. And you're a bully."

Jon smiled. "You're right."

"And you snore."

He nodded his head once. "Guilty as charged."

She glared at him, and he placed his hand low on her back, escorting her through the visitors' parking lot toward the building. "Lily, be honest with me. How many times in the past week have you been dizzy? How often have your pupils dilated like that? You swear you haven't hit your head or taken any sort of pharmaceutical, and I'm trusting you."

"Gee. Thanks."

"But I'm not going to let you do anything that might worsen whatever it is that's causing this."

"*Stress* is causing this, Agent Patrick. I told you. It started after I saw the kittens. It will end as soon as you nail this bastard. So let's go let you nail him."

It amused him; that they were already squabbling like a couple. But he had felt her muscles tense when he touched her, and he knew that no matter how light her tone might be, there was something she wasn't telling him. Something more than could be explained by the circumstances. And something *definitely* happened back there in the shelter. Not only her spell, but the reaction of the cats. When they calmed down, she calmed down. Or was it the other way around?

He'd get it out of her. Later. When he wasn't on the clock. For now, he had to think of the case, and only the case. Everything, everyone else, had to wait. Starting now. He took his worry about her condition and their chemistry, and everything even remotely Lily-shaped except for the potential of a connection between her and the Serpent, and put it into a box and closed the lid firmly.

"Jon, if you would just—"

"Lily, I told you—"

"Hey! Somebody grab that bastard!" A man's shout, annoyed but not really worried.

Patrick turned in the direction of the shout, only to feel something slug him in the chest, knocking the air out of him. He bent over, catching a glimpse out of the corner of his eye of a shadow looming over him.

"Grab him!" the voice yelled again. "Grab the son of a bitch!"

Patrick was more than willing to, as soon as he could stand up again. Then he heard another voice yelling, "Get off of me!"

Lily sounded more pissed off than scared, but instinct took over even as he was realizing that, and he had his gun out of its holster and was turning to aim at the figure clad in black jeans and hoodie. In work mode

Patrick's well-trained brain took in the instant basics: solid build, white, five-eight or so, shaking as if he had a bad case of the d.t.'s, but with a chokehold on Lily, his other hand snaking around to reach for the purse dangling from her left shoulder.

"Lily, down!" he yelled, unable to get a clear shot while she was struggling with their assailant. Damn it, damn it, damn it!

Instead of going down, she threw her head back, knocking hard against the man's face. The guy dropped her, and looked up to see a federal agent's gun aiming at him.

Kill him, something shouted in Patrick's brain. *He threatened her! Shoot him!* But a cooler, better-trained control remained, and his finger stayed on the safety, not the trigger.

The guy snarled, frustration contorting his pale, drawn-looking face into something barely human, and rushed him: a crazy movement, a desperate movement. At the last moment possible, Patrick flipped his grip so that the butt of the gun came into contact with the guy's head. Two blows were what it took to drop him, and Patrick made a mental note to give Lily half the credit for the collar.

Only then did he hear the sound of feet running on the pavement toward them, and shouting. Unmistakable, the sound of cops on the move.

"I got him, I got him, Jesus, the guy just freaked on us!"

Only then did Patrick notice that the man's hands were cuffed in front of him. That was what had hurt so much, when the guy nailed him.

"You should have gone peacefully into booking," he told the body at his feet, even as he holstered his gun and turned to check on Lily.

"We're making a bad habit of this sort of—Lily!"

She was still on her knees, blood flowing down the side of her face. "Lily?" He went to her, using his sleeve to blot the blood away.

"Bastard hit me!" She sounded so outraged, he almost laughed.

"He hit me, too," he said, feeling the blow all over again.

"Yeah, but…that's your job! Nobody hits me! How dare he! How dare he raise a hand to me!"

"Lily?" He hesitated. Anger was a normal-enough reaction to being mugged, but…her voice sounded… different. Strange. Thinner, more nasal. Had the guy broken her nose? Was she having a reaction to her earlier weirdness in the station? Jesus, he should have insisted that she go directly to the hospital, do not pass go, do not… He placed his hands gently on either side of her face, trying to get a better look at where the blood was coming from. The frission of pleasure that came from touching her was muted by the warm drip of blood. Scalp wound probably. But… "Lily, look at me."

She drew away, as though affronted. "Who are you? Where is My Lord? How dare you touch me?"

"What?" He gaped at her, and then looked over his shoulder. "Hey, someone, get a paramedic here, stat!" Two dozen cops and not one of them useful.

"Take this idiot inside and book him," he heard a

gruff voice say, and then the scuffle of their assailant being taken away.

"Moron." It wasn't clear if the cop was talking about the criminal or the cop who hadn't been able to control him. "Sorry about that. I swear, it was like he saw you guys and totally flipped out. Ambulance is already on the way. Check both of you out, make sure everything's okay."

"I'm fine," Patrick said. The guy had hit him hard with the metal bracelets, but nothing was broken or otherwise in need of taping up. He'd cracked enough ribs in his time to know what that felt like. "Lily…she got knocked in the head." All right, technically she had knocked her head into the prep. Not a useful distinction right now.

There was a siren and the heavy crunch of the ambulance; the EMTs wasted no time when the call came in from the police station.

"Oh God. God. What's…?" She was looking at her hands, flexing them, fingertips into her palms, shaking her head back and forth. "My fingers feel funny. They itch. And burn."

"Ma'am?" A paramedic squatted next to her, reaching out with a cautious hand to get Lily's attention.

"What's happening to me? Where am I? How dare he lay hands on me?"

The paramedic looked up at Patrick, who shrugged, feeling unutterably helpless. "The guy rushed us, grabbed her. She gave him a serious head butt…"

"That'll knock some confusion into ya, yeah. What's her name?"

"Lily. Lily Malkin."

"Ms. Malkin? We need to get that bleeding stopped, is that okay? We're going to take you to the hospital and patch you up, make sure everything's working okay. You good with that?"

"Jon?"

Her voice was soft, thin, and it hurt worse than the mugger's fist. But the box's lid held tight. He couldn't, wouldn't, give in. The clock was ticking, and the Serpent was still out there, waiting. Threatening.

"You go with him, Lily-kit. I'll go get this guy, and it'll all be over."

Lily didn't remember much about the trip to the hospital. A lot of questions, and fuzzy-outlined men in faded white uniforms, and sirens that made her skull want to shatter until she started to cry, and they made the driver turn it off.

Then they were there, and she was being unloaded into the E.R. It was surprisingly, blessedly quiet. Lily was stripped of her jeans and sweater, the items going wherever her coat had already disappeared to, and wrapped in a flimsy paper robe that barely wrapped around, but came down her knees.

It bothered her that she couldn't stop her fingers from curling and uncurling. A nervous twitch, and if the doctors saw it, they'd sedate her, try to keep her. Lily didn't mind doctors, but she didn't want to be here. Not now. Now with her brain all fuzzy and noisy, like a radio station picking up two different signals and only one speaker.

"Hush." The static gave her the finger, and continued. "Ms. Malkin?"

"Yes." She looked up to greet the doctor. He had a clipboard and an air of competence that she found reassuring, even if he did seem barely twenty.

"All right, let's take a look at you, shall we?" He stepped closer, and removed a light pen from his coat pocket. "Look up, please?"

Lily hesitated, and then looked up.

"Well…" He paused. "How's your vision?"

"Okay. The light's sort of weird, but no blurriness or blind spots." The paramedics had asked her the same thing.

"And you haven't…"

"Taken any drugs or alcohol, no." Telling him that her eyes had been doing that on and off all week probably wouldn't help her get out of there, so she didn't. And she hid her fingers in the flimsy paper cloth of her exam gown.

The doctor went ahead and checked her vitals, finding nothing particularly off kilter. Her reflexes were, in his words, fabulous, she didn't have a headache, and he didn't notice the way her fingers kept flexing. She didn't tell them about the ache in her fingertips, either.

"All right, let me go check up on your X-rays. I'll be right back."

She sat on the edge of the cot and waited, her legs swinging annoyingly in the air. Who designed these exam rooms, anyway, the Jolly Green Giant? God, while she waited here, who knew what was happening out there? What had Jon found?

A nurse walked by, and she reached out to grab at her sleeve. "Where's a phone?"

"Excuse me?"

Lily mimed picking up a receiver and dialing. "A phone?"

"There's one down the hallway…oh, no, it's broken." The nurse frowned. "You don't have a cell phone?"

"Never needed one," Lily said, cranky. Why did everyone assume everyone else felt the need to be in touch at all times? All she wanted was to make a simple phone call. And her purse was off somewhere with the rest of her belongings, she realized. The cops had taken it as evidence, or something. "Never mind. I don't have any change on me anyway."

"I'll tell you what. Let me get a chair, and we can let you use the phone at the desk. Okay?"

Lily tried to smile at the woman who was, after all, trying to help. They grabbed a wheelchair from the hallway and the nurse—Georgia, according to her name tag—pushed her to the nurses' station, where a quick conversation with the woman behind the desk got a heavy sigh and access to a phone.

Lily closed her eyes and tried to remember Jon's number. She usually had an excellent memory for numbers, but…there it was.

"This is Special Agent Jon T. Patrick. Leave your name, number and a brief message, and I will return your call as soon as I am able."

Lily put down the phone and thanked the nurses numbly. There were a lot of reasons why his phone wasn't picking up. He might be in a warehouse, or a basement. Somewhere a signal didn't get through. That happened, didn't it? Even to FBI-issue cell phones? No reason to assume anything was wrong.

"You okay, hon?" Georgia wasn't that much older than her, if at all, but her concern had a definite maternal feel to it, and suddenly Lily wanted to cry. Her own mother had died when she was a child, and while her father had loved her, he wasn't exactly the sort to use nicknames or endearments.

"Yeah. I just…" Just what? Was upset because her Fibbie wasn't answering his phone? That he was more concerned with the stats of his case than her well-being? He had shoved her off to the paramedics fast enough, not even letting a mugging slow him down.

Lily was angry but she wasn't sure why. At Jon, Special Agent Patrick, for thinking of the case before her? Or herself, for letting it matter? She had no claim on him, and he had no obligation to her.

"We need to get you back to the cubicle," Georgia said, turning the chair around and pushing Lily back to her cubicle. "Doctor will be here soon, not good to have him thinking you slipped out on him. Gives them complexes when that happens. Fragile egos, these doctors."

"Ah, there you are. Georgia, what have I told you about kidnapping our patients?"

Georgia helped Lily out of the chair and back onto the cot, not giving the doctor the benefit of a response. "You hang in there, hon."

"Thank you."

"So." The doctor consulted his clipboard, and then looked directly at her, as though he had already memorized everything he needed to say. "Your X-rays show nothing wrong. Your heart rate is elevated slightly, but nothing that is out of place for what you've been through. You have, as expected, a concussion. The pupil enlargement is worrying, but without anything setting off alarms.... I'm willing to release you so long as there is someone to drive you home and stay with you for the next twenty-four hours."

There was a dry cough from just outside the cubicle's heavy white curtains, where Officer Stephens was unapologetically, part-of-the-job-ma'am eavesdropping.

"I have a police escort," Lily said dryly. "I think I'm okay."

After the doctor ascertained that yes, Officer Stephens was there for the sole purpose of making sure she didn't fall down and go boom again, and would stay with her until a family member could arrive, he agreed to release her into the gentle care of Newfield's finest.

They brought her her clothing and drew the curtains for privacy. She managed to get re-dressed without too much difficulty, but her sweater snagged on a finger-nail and the threads dragged out, making her swear un-happily and without much enthusiasm. She had never been very good at cursing.

Lily finally got her shoes on and laced them up, then pushed the curtain aside to interrupt Stephens and the doctor still talking.

"I'll be right back." She was moving slow, but her feet were steady under her, the walls weren't doing the woobly thing again, and everything smelled and sounded normal. She made it to the phone at the nurses' station and looked at the woman behind the counter with the best pitiful expression she could manage.

It must have been pretty effective, because the desk-bound nurse just waved a hand at the phone as though to say "have at it."

She could recall the number easily now. But the result was the same: it went directly to voice mail.

She should have gone back to Stephens's custody, had him drive her home, taken the pills they were going to give her and settled in on her sofa with a blanket wrapped around her, surfing the TV. Maybe she'd order food and invite the boys in. It would be the least she could do.

Come to me.

Maybe she would have him stop on the way home and pick up a few movie rentals. Something to keep her mind off whatever was going on with Jon. Keep her from worrying about whatever was happening to her, which couldn't be anything because the doctors didn't find anything. Something to de-stress by. A romantic comedy maybe, or a Marx Brothers movie.

Come to me.

Lily shook her head, trying to dislodge the odd whisper she kept hearing. She just wanted to go home, that was all. Go home, and have Agent Patrick call her and say he'd gotten the guy, that he would never hurt another cat again, never call her house or break into another cattery. And then Agent Patrick would return to Washington, and she could get her life back under control.

Without conscious volition, Lily moved away from the nurses' desk, across the lobby to where a large picture window would have let in sunlight during the day. The hospital was built into part of a hill, so they were raised above ground level slightly, even though the E.R. was technically on the first floor.

She looked into the sky, noting that the moon was almost finished waning. The end of the week would be the new moon, when the sky would be lit only by the distant stars.

Come to me. I need you.

She looked down, as though searching for the source of the whisper. A half-moon driveway, with an ambulance waiting outside, and beyond that a parking lot, cast into shadows by the streetlights.

A smaller, more distinct shadow moved by the ambulance, catching her attention. A man, half hidden, looking up into the window.

Looking at *her.*

I need you. Come home.

She couldn't see his face at that distance. And yet, she knew it. Lean and regal, black hair oiled back off the high forehead, a hawk's nose and black eyes that saw everything and valued far less.

It looked nothing like the face in the drawing they had shown her. But she knew him. The Night Serpent.

And then she remembered. Everything.

Chapter 14

"Ms. Malkin?"

Lily turned to see Officer Stephens standing there, her coat and purse over his arm. "They just need you to sign some paperwork. I'll go get the car, okay?"

"Yes. Thank you."

She looked back, but the figure was gone. Had it even been there? She was operating on autopilot, her body moving and her mouth talking while her mind was somewhere else entirely. All the nightmares, the shadowed hallucinations, the voices, the strange unease and desires she felt…

All real. And impossible.

You are not who you are.

Impossible.

You are the Superior of the Guardians of the Children of Bastet.

Impossible.

And yet the memories flooded her, the solid pain each one brought proof that impossible did not mean unreal.

…Dancing in the gardens under Her approving eye…

…grooming a sleek spotted cat, its head resting trustingly on her bare forearm, the rumble of its purr a blessing from Herself…

…the appearance of a man in the temple, seeking wisdom and guidance…

…hushed conversations, avoiding the attentions of the beasts she had once catered to, guilt-stricken as she did what her lover asked of her, never asking why he asked, why she gave….

…the heat of her lover's gaze as he touched her…the heat of his gaze as he repudiated her, betrayed her, murdered her….

That thought stilled her.

Murdered. She had been murdered, the blood pooling on the cool stone floor, her body left for the temple beasts to discover.

Lily shuddered, feeling the information break over her, drowning her, even as her body left the hospital, got into the car, was driven away.

Murdered?

You betrayed them first. You gave Her secrets to an outsider. For what?

For love. The memory of a face again. Dark, intense eyes burning with need. Ambition.

For love unrequited. The need was not for you, but power. He used you for his own ambition. And you died for it. Died unjustified, cast off by the Mother and forbidden peace by all the gods…

Eight lives passed behind her eyes, all lived so much as this current one had been, with hesitation and uncertainty, alone and afraid… Each life a cycle of the same choices, the same failures, century after century. Never able to trust, to make the leap, to break the cycle. Always ending in failure.

Until this life. Until the day she moved to Newfield. The day she stepped inside the cat shelter, determined to overcome her fear. That had made the difference, she was certain of it.

There is something I'm supposed to do. Something important. But I don't know how. Or when.

Another dream-memory, recent this time. A lean, elegant tawny cat, its pelt covered with black spots, sitting in a classic temple pose. Pale olive-green eyes staring at her, the pupil growing larger and larger until she was about to fall into them.

"The Night Serpent." She spoke out loud without realizing it.

Stephens took his eyes off the road and looked at her. "Yeah?"

"He said…that I knew. That I could tell him… what?"

Her escort turned his attention back to the road. "Ms. Malkin, you can't think too hard about what crazy folk say. Leave that to people like Agent Patrick. He specializes in crazy."

Lily absorbed that. Yes. He did. And did that explain his fascination for her? Was she crazy, too? Was that why the Night Serpent found her, because they were both crazy together? Had they met before, in previous lives? The connection Jon had spoken about. Cat-scratch crazy.

It didn't make any sense, otherwise, all of it. Her life was quiet, contained. And now, suddenly, she was stalked, mugged, escorted by cops, having fabulous sex with a guy she'd only known a week....

And convinced that she'd lived another life before this one. A number of lives, actually. Eight, to be precise.

This was her ninth.

She was out of lives.

And she had no idea, still, what she was supposed to do.

Come home.

The Night Serpent knew.

"Hey."

"What?" She practically jumped out of her seat, held in place only by the seat belt.

Stephens was looking at her oddly. "We're here."

They had pulled onto her street without her even noticing. She struggled to control the things in her head, shoving them away so that she had time and room to think.

The cop saw her struggle, but misunderstood the cause. "The doc said he gave you a prescription for something for stress, help you relax. I forgot to ask if you wanted to drop it off at the drugstore to be filled— should we go back?"

Lily touched her shoulder bag almost reflexively, reassuring herself that the slip of paper was still in there. "No. I don't think so." It was tempting: take a pill, make everything go away. No more stress, no more hallucinations, no more weird freaky feelings or eyesight problems or feeling as if she was about to slide out of her own skin... Except it would still all be there. She just wouldn't care so much.

She had the feeling that it was important to care. It was important to remember.

"You sure? No offense, Ms. Malkin, but you look like you could use something, and I'm thinking you're not much for a knockback of whiskey."

She almost smiled at that. No, she wasn't much of a drinker, other than the occasional glass of wine or beer with dinner. She didn't think she even had any alcohol in the house, except for some cooking sherry.

But she said the only thing that he might understand. "I'd rather keep my head clear."

Stephens pulled into her driveway, hesitated, then turned to her without turning off the engine. "About five years ago. My partner and I were involved in a shooting downtown. Totally justified, I did everything by the book, but for a while I had the shakes pretty bad. Took time off, went on some meds the doctor suggested when things got too bad. I was scared it would screw with me, make me not able to do my job? But...it helped me do my job, on the bad days. I wasn't trying to second-guess what was a real doubt, and what was a stress-memory."

That hit home, quivering like an arrow thunking into flesh. She had never talked about that with her therapist, had never thought to ask. "How do you tell the difference? Between real and…stress?"

He shrugged. "You have to trust yourself. And accept that mistakes are gonna happen, but if they do, you're gonna take responsibility for them too."

"Yeah." Lily leaned her head back against the seat and closed her eyes, willing the quivering to go away. "That's always the trick, isn't it?" She shook her head, smiled and reached over to unhook her seat belt. "I'll think about it. That's all I can promise."

Stephens turned off the engine and got out of the car in time to help her out of her own seat. "And if all else fails," he said only half jokingly, "there's always whiskey."

She shook her head as he escorted her to the door.

"Thank you for the ride home. But you're off duty. You don't really have to…"

"Ms. Malkin. Even if I were willing to leave you alone after getting mugged in *our* parking lot, Detective Petrosian would have my—" he started to say one thing, and then switched midthought "—badge in a minute if I didn't make sure you were okay until Agent Patrick got here."

Her eyes narrowed, and the itch in her fingers came back with a vengeance. Even as she knew her anger was probably unwarranted, she let it come, relishing in the outrage. "Has this all been worked out then? That the helpless female has a keeper at all times?"

Stephens might not have been married, but he knew when he'd overstepped. He also knew his job. And nobody would ever fault his bravery.

"No, ma'am. But you have a concussion. If you want

to call a friend to stay with you instead, that's fine. But I will wait until they arrive."

Lily stared at him, his crew cut and square jaw making him look like a grown-up Cub Scout. She could call half a dozen people; she had people—not many, but Ronnie and Aggie—who would drop everything if they heard she had been injured and needed help. But if she did that, asked for help, they would assume she was worse off than she actually was, and they would never leave her be, after. Stephens, at least, knew the limits of the job.

And if Agent Patrick did show up? After abandoning her to the E.R., turning off his phone, ignoring her for hours? Too much. Too much to handle right now. They'd deal with that if and when it happened.

"Did you get anything to eat at the hospital? All I've got are leftovers, but we should be able to put together something reasonably healthy." She hung her coat in the closet and went into the kitchen. If he was going to play nanny, he could hang up his own coat.

"There's…brown rice and sesame chicken. Some salad. Half a parm—"

The radio at Stephens's hip squawked, and he tabbed it on, listening to whatever was being reported. Lily felt herself tense, the hand on the refrigerator door tightening until the knuckles turned white. Her fingertips tingled again, and she felt a faint burn, as though the skin was splitting under her nails.

Stephens came into the kitchen, and she forced herself to go back to inspecting the contents of the fridge. "What happened?" It wasn't Jon. It wasn't. She would not allow it to be….

"Shooting." Lily's gut tightened with cold fear until he continued, "Down by the Bridges." A series of interlocked pedestrian walkways over the river, by the park. Not the best neighborhood. "Somebody took potshots at a patrol car." He shook his head, resigned but not worried. "Every now and again, the gene pool gets cleaned out."

"Idiots," she said in agreement, feeling her chest begin to expand and contract again. "So, you want—"

The doorbell rang.

"You expecting someone?" she asked Stephens. Maybe it was Dunkirk or one of the other cops on drive-by duty, stopping by for coffee. They didn't, as a rule, but you never knew....

He shook his head again, and motioned her to stand closer to the refrigerator. Stephens went to the door, right hand by his hip, near where his gun was holstered. He approached the door sideways, looking out the side window. The tension released, and he went to open the door.

"Agent Patrick."

"People who turn off their cell phones and don't call don't get any dinner," Lily sang out, suddenly feeling reckless. He was alive. He was safe. He was an utter bastard for abandoning her like that, casting her...

Casting her aside in order to focus on his job.

"You have no more use to me. They will never trust you again, once it is discovered what you did. But the man who brings the betrayer to justice, he will be rewarded beyond measure...."

Her lover's face, shadowed and cruel. She reached

for him, tried to touch him, to bring him back to her. Then there was a hot blow to her side, and a cold red haze crept over her eyes....

"No."

"Lily?" Jon was at her side, and she stared blankly at him. The man she had seen outside the hospital had looked nothing like the man suspected of being the Night Serpent. But his eyes, his face...

He looked an awful lot like one Jon T. Patrick.

Laughter—more than slightly hysterical—bubbled up inside her. Never say she didn't have a type....

"Lily?" Jon looked over his shoulder at Stephens, who was reaching for his coat, the very picture of a man getting the hell out of the way. Petrosian was behind him, closing the front door against the night chill.

"You didn't get him." She wasn't looking at him. What was wrong?

"No. But we found his lair."

"More dead cats?' Her voice sounded...flat. Monotone.

"No cats at all. No real ones, anyway. There was... Lily, are you all right?"

"Yes. I'm fine. The doctor said so."

Ow. Patrick winced. He had meant to get back to her, to meet her at the hospital, but the things they had discovered at the site had to be dealt with right away. Lily wanted the guy caught; she understood that had to be priority. Didn't she?

He sucked at relationships. He always had. And when had this suddenly become a relationship? What had happened to some fun sex with a lovely and willing woman?

And who the hell was he trying to kid? He would have laughed, except it would have gone down completely wrong, and possibly gotten him killed with a kitchen knife.

The words the cop had said in the parking lot came back to him. "It was like he saw you and flipped." The guy was a meth-head, fried and finished. Maybe he looked like an old teacher who'd flunked the guy, or Lily like an old girlfriend who dumped him. There was no way there was a connection between some random junkie and this case.

There was no way the Serpent had somehow lured them to the police station, set that guy on them, to harm Lily, to separate them. That was… Crazy.

"Sir?" Stephens beckoned to him and, with a worried look at Lily, who was busy pulling cartons out of the fridge, he went back to speak with the two cops. A quick update on what the doctor had said, and Lily's comments on the trip back to the house, caught Patrick up.

Something was wrong. Something was…crazy. Right now, he wasn't discounting anything, and he wasn't taking any more chances.

"Thanks. And thank you," he said to Stephens. "Go home and get some rest. We'll take over for tonight."

By the time he got back to the kitchen, Lily had a platter piled with an assortment of leftovers, and was placing it in the microwave.

"I assume you didn't have dinner."

"Or lunch," he said in agreement. "And I'm an ass."

"Yes. You are."

Her voice was still flat. He wanted to protect her, keep her safe. He also wanted to tell her what they had found, get her take on it. He wanted that lovely brain that went with the lovely body. But he didn't know where to begin, with this monosyllabic, quiet-voiced woman who was so clearly pissed at him. Somehow, he didn't think that running down to the quick-mart for flowers was going to do the trick.

The detective, having seen Stephens out the door, came back into the kitchen. "Hey, Aggie," she said in greeting, still in that monotone voice.

"Lily. You scared the hell out of me, girl."

Petrosian got a smile for that, and Patrick felt an unexpected pang of jealousy hit him. Jealousy, and anger—why did the older man get a smile, and he got the freeze-out? He had apologized....

Maybe flowers were the way to go. Not lilies, though.

The microwave went off, and the moment was lost. The next few minutes were an almost comfortable fuss of getting glasses, platter and plates to the table. But once everyone settled themselves with the food, he felt the awkward silence return.

It was a marked contrast to their first meal together, when he had actively pursued, and she had been cautiously amused. Now he felt as though he were walking on a minefield, and she...

He had no idea what she was right now.

"The doctor gave you a clean bill of health, Stephens

said." Her eyes looked normal, the few times she'd let him catch her gaze. She was twitchy, though: her fingers closed over her fork as though she wasn't quite sure how to hold it, and her head kept cocking to the side, as though she was listening for something.

"Yes. Physically, I'm fine. What did you find?" The question was directed to Petrosian.

The cop looked over at Patrick, and then shrugged. "Weird. I'm not any kind of expert on crazy, but this seemed pretty textbook. Empty—he'd skedaddled, probably just before we got there. But all his stuff was there. He was building some kind of archway, all draped in black. A couple of stuffed cats, the taxidermy kind of stuffed, the ones that are meant to look cute but are just creepy? Like he was using them as placeholders or something, moving them around until he was satisfied it looked right. And there was a statue, a cat statue, made of—get this—foam, and spray painted black, too. A bunch of symbols on the wall, chalked outlines, like he hadn't gotten around to filling them in yet."

"Symbols? You mean something satanic?"

"Not quite," Patrick said. "Hieroglyphics. Egyptian."

Her eyes flickered to him, and then back to Petrosian, but in that instant Patrick saw something in them, something that set him on edge, set off all of his alarms, both professional and personal.

Fear. No—terror.

Chapter 15

Lily excused herself to go use the bathroom. Once there, she rested her forehead against the closed door and let herself give in to the shudders.

Egyptian. Of course.

She couldn't deny it any longer. Whatever was happening, whatever had brought the Night Serpent to her town, and into her life…she was the cause. Or the catalyst. Or somehow responsible in a way she couldn't avoid.

She had to tell them.

"Oh sure, right," she said, hearing the near hysteria edging back into her voice. "This guy? He's here because of me. Only, not the me I was. Or something that's trying to get through, using me. I don't know what. But I have memories, and he thinks because of that I know something he needs.

"How does he know? What, do I look like I have the answers?

"Oh, and Agent Patrick? I don't trust you worth a damn, either. Except I don't have any choice but to trust you."

Hysteria. Definitely.

She splashed water on her face, dried it roughly to bring some color to her skin and stared at herself in the mirror.

Black hair. Hazel eyes. Skin more golden than pale. She had always thought that she looked like her father's side of the family, a mixture of Italian and Spanish. The snub nose and rounded chin were from her mother.

She didn't know what an Egyptian might look like. Mummies were all she knew about that country. Mummies, and pyramids, and things blowing up on the news, and…

Bast. Bastet. The cat-headed goddess.

She knew more about the goddess than she should. If she would only let herself completely remember.

But if she did, if she let the memories come back over her—where would Lily go?

That was the thought that terrified her.

Where would Lily go if she was someone else, as well?

By the time she came back, the guys had cleared the table, and the coffee machine had been started. Jon. It should have been nice, having someone feel so comfortable in her home. It wasn't.

Nothing felt nice right now.

The guys were sitting in the living room, photos spread out over the coffee table in front of them. The television was on, turned to the 11:00 p.m. news, the sound turned low. A reporter was standing in front of the Newfield Zoo. A follow-up to the break-in. Lily hoped that nobody got hurt—Jon hadn't told her. Jon—Agent Patrick—hadn't told her shit. She liked the sound of the swearword. Shit. She felt like saying it out loud, but didn't.

"We sent e-files to the office," Patrick was saying. "There are specialists they can work with to see if there's anything we're missing. But right now I'm building a case that this guy is fixated on ancient Egypt specifically for the cats."

"They were considered holy back then," Lily said, sitting down on the sofa next to her lover. She was still angry with him. But she wanted to be near him, too. "Killing a cat was considered murder, and families went into mourning when a pet died. They shaved their eyebrows."

"Really?" Petrosian raised his own shaggy brows.

"So he's killing them in front of a statue of a cat-headed goddess…and this one—" Jon pointed to one of the photos showing a close-up of a statue of a man with the head of a jackal "—that's Osiris, god of the underworld. He judged the dead, decided if—"

"That was Anubis," she corrected him.

"What?"

"Anubis. He weighed the soul against a feather. It had to balance before a soul could move on to its reward."

Jon looked at the photo, then back at her. "What happened if it didn't balance?"

Lily stared at the photos, but couldn't bring herself to answer.

Ma'at. The word came to her, a match lit in the darkness. Truth. Harmony. *Justice.*

But justice for whom? Was that what the Night Serpent was saying, that she should know? Was the Night Serpent there for her? To bring her to justice for a sin committed lifetimes ago?

Or was she the one who had to bring *him* into harmony? Impossible to know. Impossible, period. One thing she did know: he was looking for her. And that couldn't be good.

"All right." Lily came back to the conversation that had continued while she zoned. "So he's gone from killing cats to killing cats in a ritual manner, to killing and building an arch, and you think that he's invoking, or trying to reach, an Egyptian god or gods?"

"Short version—he's a nut."

Jon grimaced at Petrosian's summation, echoing Lily's comment days ago. "But he's a nut with a plan. And one that involves Lily somehow. Or he wants it to, or thinks it needs to. Whatever he's doing isn't working, and because of her connection with cats in the media's eyes, he's focusing on her as having the solution."

"He thinks I know what he's doing wrong." It wasn't a question, but Jon treated it that way.

"Probably. He seems to have a fixation on cats, so you're an authority figure in his eyes. 'She knows' he said—he thinks that you know what this goddess wants.

It makes sense—your skills with cats, and a female cat-headed god…."

Lily, frustrated, shook her head hard enough that her hair came out of her barrette. He was so close, but there was no way he could make the leap to the truth. Not without her telling him, and she couldn't. Not without coming across as a total crazy herself.

"Except that it sounds like he's claiming that she— Bast—is giving him information, that she told him to find me. That doesn't make any sense. She's associated with cats in a positive way, and he's killing them."

"I don't think he sees it that way," Jon said. "He was taking good care of them before they died. Food, shelter. None of them were abused or injured. And they trusted him enough to rest quietly while he cut their throats, without any kind of drugs or restraints."

Lily shivered, suddenly cold despite the heat coming up through the vents. That connection thing again that Jon had mentioned. They must think that this guy, the Night Serpent, was a cat talker, too. Connected to Bast, somehow. That was why the cats hadn't fought him, but laid down to die.

A connection. Another connection between them. The cats should be fighting him, not giving way. What had he done?

She stood and went into the kitchen to check on the coffee. It was ready, so she loaded up a tray with mugs, sugar, milk and the coffeepot, and—balancing it all carefully—went back into the living room. Petrosian stood and took it from her, obviously worried she was going to pass out again and drop his coffee on the floor.

Jon had gotten up and was pacing, thinking out loud and waving his hand as though lecturing. "He's not harming the cats, in his eyes. He's sacrificing them. Sending them on to…this cat-headed goddess—Bast? He wants something from her, her and this other god, Anubis or Osiris or whatever. But it's not working. He's starting to get desperate. And that's when we've got him. The moment he stops thinking and starts reacting."

"Patrick. No." Petrosian saw where that was heading.

"What?" Lily put her coffee down and stared at Jon. "What are you thinking?"

"You aren't gonna like it," Petrosian warned her. He clearly didn't, anyway.

Agent Patrick stopped in front of Lily, crouching in front of her. His dark eyes were shadowed; he hadn't been sleeping much, either. Not all of that was her fault. They had slept, after. For a little while.

"There weren't any cats at his last hiding spot," he said as though trying to convince her of something. "No cages, even. Just the setup, more elaborate than before. Larger. Like it was a taunt." His eyes met her, and she read the knowledge in them: they both knew that the call-in had been fake, that they had been meant to find that lair. Meant to have the knowledge. But only Lily knew why.

"He may still have his breeding queens, but the way his sacrifices have sped up, he thinks that he's running out of time. Or he's got a deadline of some kind," Patrick went on. "If so, he's screwed. The Serpent believes that he needs the cats to be of a certain age, and a specific color and pattern. He tried to steal some that fit the requirements, he's tried to adopt some, and he's been blocked at every end. That run at the zoo— he might have been crazy enough to try for a leopard or something, before the rent-a-cops showed up."

"If it was him," Petrosian objected. "We don't know that for certain."

"It was him," Lily said, not liking the cold feeling of certainty in her gut. "If he really thinks that he's reaching Bast, or touched by her, or whatever crazies believe, maybe he also believed that he could get his hands on a leopard or something without getting turned into dinner?"

"Or he wanted you to do it," Jon said, putting into words exactly what she didn't want to hear.

"Are you crazy?" Lily shook her head, denying it. "I'm just, okay, yeah, the cat lady." She hated the title even more now. "Those things? The great cats? They weigh more than I do, and have claws like dinner knifes, and—"

"They're cats," Petrosian said, reluctantly agreeing with Patrick. "Like that one you dealt with in the apartment complex."

"And I had half a dozen cops with guns backing me up. Anyway, an ocelot is *not* a tiger."

"And a house cat isn't an ocelot. But you did it. If this guy knows that… Maybe he didn't want you to do it, just to show him how. That could have been what he meant. He's stronger than you are, being a guy…." Agent Patrick was back in control, thinking out loud.

Lily felt ill. "They got them all back though, right? The cats?"

"What? Oh, yeah, all safe and sound, and they only lost a few antelope in the process." He tried for a reassuring smile. She didn't buy it, but appreciated the effort.

"Whatever he's been trying, it's not enough," she said. "You think that he went after a big cat, maybe thinking more would be more effective? He's afraid that he's not doing the right thing...."

"Or the sacrifice wasn't the right kind. Oh God, I hope he hasn't made that jump."

"Jump? What jump? Jump to what?" Lily wasn't quite sure she was following his thoughts, and she wasn't sure she wanted to, either, not with the look on his face.

"He thinks this guy's going to go after the cat lady next," Aggie said bluntly, his hound dog face looking even more mournful than usual. "Not just a person of interest—a part of his whacked out plan. Cat-headed goddess. Cat-talking woman. Guy said it himself; he thinks you know what he's supposed to be doing. Maybe if you can't explain it to him, you get to graduate to *being* the sacrifice."

She had been following him, then. She'd been afraid of that.

"To the Night Serpent, to his internal logic, it would make sense," Patrick said in his cool FBI-guy voice, as if it was all theory and happening to someone else.

It made sense to Lily, too. But for reasons other than Jon's crazy-person-thinks-like-that logic. If he knew what she…had been, then how much more useful a sacrifice she would be than cats, degraded over centuries from their temple origins.

He had already killed her at least once. What was one more?

"Either way, his fascination with you might be to our benefit." Patrick was still talking. "Especially if he's starting to speed up and panic."

"You want to use her as bait." Aggie was working up a good pissed-off.

"You used her already," Patrick retorted, not denying the accusation. "You brought her into this, not me. You're the one who got her into the media's eye!"-The FBI voice was gone, stripped down to…fear?

"Hey!" Lily's shout cut into whatever Aggie was going to respond. "I'm here. I'm not a chunk of meat to be fought over by two chest-thumping male apes. Okay?"

"She's already bait," Jon said more quietly, almost under control again. "The media made sure of that. Or have you forgotten why your men are patrolling the area?"

Petrosian glared, but had no comeback.

"Your food's getting cold, Aggie," Lily said quietly. "Eat."

He picked up his fork, and then pointed it at her. "You don't have to agree to his schemes, Lily. I'm not going to carry around guilt for bringing him in if you do anything stupid."

"I'm not going to agree to anything stupid," she told him. "But he's right. The Night Serpent wants to talk to me. If we can use that to catch him… I have a responsibility to do it." It was her way out; she could do what she needed to do, and not have to risk telling them anything. She didn't have to risk Jon looking at her, not with sexual interest, but professional curiosity: one of the crazy people. Something to use.

Or, if he was going to use her, let it be on her terms. This time she would get something out of it, for herself. No more being a tool to be discarded the moment the job was done.

Not that she really believed she had lived previous lives. That was…insane. But something was happening. And she had a responsibility because of it. Or despite it. She could stop any more cats from being killed if they caught this guy. And if Jon's theory was right, maybe stop any people from ever getting killed.

Including herself. Again.

"Not without backup," Aggie was saying, having accepted that she was serious. "I'll have the depart-ment—"

"And I'll be able to call an official backup for this. Plus, we can use the media…" Jon started to say.

She held up a hand to stop their words. "I don't care. You figure something out. I'll do it. For now, I've had a really long day, the painkillers are wearing off, and I'm going to bed. Aggie, I'll see you tomorrow. Jon, either lock up before or after yourself, your call. Good night."

She woke up three times to darkness, her breath gasping, and cold sweat pooling between her shoulder blades and the backs of her knees.

The third time there was a warm presence next to her, solid and reassuring, even as he hogged most of the blankets. She had heard him in the living room, talking on his cell to someone back in D.C., when exhaustion finally claimed her. Apparently even Fibbie endurance had its limits. She curled on her side, facing her lover, and reached out to touch the shadowed skin of his shoulder.

Shadows. So many shadows, inside and out. Her mind was not letting her rest, unable to let go of the questions there were no answers for. As usual, she did not remember her nightmares, but the shadows remained, along with the image of a cat watching her. Asking the impossible of her. She woke each time asking the same things, over and over again.

Who was the Night Serpent? A deranged man playing out some sick fantasy of power that made sense only to himself? Or was he…

She skirted around the thought, but was unable to avoid it entirely.

Or was he the reincarnation of an ancient Egyptian, a man of high status, who used and cast aside people on his quest for more and more power? A murderer, without conscience or guilt?

Or…her mind skittered further from the thought, until she held it down firmly and faced it. The fact that the man in her visions, the man she saw outside the hospital, looked nothing at all like the man suspected of being the Night Serpent. And everything like one Special Agent Jon T. Patrick. A man of passion and conviction…and self-admitted ambition. A man who, though regretful, would use his lover to achieve his goal.

She let her hand rest on his shoulder, fingers curling

into his neck until her claws cut gently into the flesh, and he stirred in sleepy protest.

Could she trust him? Even if she was wrong, and he was an innocent bystander…could she trust him?

Only as she was drifting off to sleep did she suddenly realize that, although the room had been cast in darkness, she had been able to see perfectly in the faint moonlight.

Cat's eyes.

Finally, she thought, too tired and worn-down to be alarmed. Something *useful.*

Chapter 16

"The moon's almost gone," she said, looking up into the early-morning sky. The sun was still below the horizon, and the sliver of moon still held on to the pale blue expanse. Jon came behind her, wrapping his arms around her and looking out the window over her shoulder.

"The full moon is traditionally a time of higher activity for abnormal behaviors," he said, his voice muffled by the tangle of her hair.

"Not this time," she said. "The dark of the moon is what he's waiting for."

Jon's arms tightened around her slightly. "How do you know?"

"I don't know. Maybe you're right, and there is a connection between us. I..." She wanted to tell him.

She truly did. But the resemblance between him and the man in her visions was too close, too unnerving. He was fond of her, he maybe even had real feelings for her. But the woman in her not-memories had thought her lover was true, too, and had been wrong.

Lily wasn't brave enough to risk it. She only had so much courage, and what she was about to do was using every drop of it.

"I just feel that we don't have a lot of time," she said finally.

"We don't. It's been a week since his last scene. He's been escalating, building up steam, and a week is about as long as he can do without erupting now. Especially since he's refocusing on you. If he's running to pattern, he's working himself up to something, something major. Are you sure you're ready for this?"

"No. But I'm going to do it anyway."

They hadn't come up with a plan so much as a plan had come up and slapped them in the face. The day after agreeing to let her play bait, Aggie came over for dinner, and they had a brainstorming session. The TV was playing in the other room, and Lily's attention was caught by the tail end of a follow-up to the break-in at the zoo.

"The break-in was, according to officials, a professional job, and not the work, as was previously suggested, of teenagers, similar to the rash of break-ins last summer. Last night a privately owned animal park was also hit and several animals were stolen. Officials speculate that they were taken by black marketers, to be sold to so-called big-game hunters to become 'easy' trophies. From the Newfield Zoo, this is Alissa Kent, for Channel 3 News."

"Thank you, Alissa. Terrible news, just terrible. And now for the weather…"

"I never knew we had that many animal parks in town. I—" Lily stopped, looking suddenly at Jon. He had the same expression she was probably wearing: dawning, horrified suspicion. Jumping. Escalating. The killer was escalating.

Petrosian was already dialing by the time Jon reached for his cell phone.

"What do you mean you don't know what was taken? Get the damn report and check!"

"It was him. He took their cats. At least one, probably more."

"We don't know for certain…." Petrosian began, then held up a finger as whomever he had been yelling at came back with the report. "Shit. Yeah. All right, yeah. Thanks. You do that."

He closed the phone and looked at them, his heavy eyes mournful. "They had a breeding pair of cheetahs. The male's missing."

A day later, Lily had found herself in the overly warm studio of the local news show, being interviewed by a perky reporter trying for her best serious face while clearly thinking that this was nothing more than a publicity puff piece. The segment had aired this morning. They had been waiting ever since.

"Anyone want another donut?" The feds had shown up at the crack of dawn, bearing cases of electronics and serious expressions. Aggie had arrived an hour later bearing a box from Dunkin' Donuts. So far, all Lily had been able to stomach was a strawberry-filled donut and three cups of coffee. A bowl of vegetable soup sat in front of her, cooling, but she hadn't done more than poke the spoon at it.

The phone rang.

Lily froze, looking at the machine as though she had never seen it before. It was him. She knew it, the way she had known him outside the hospital. It was him, and she had no idea what to do. She wanted to run, hide, pretend that she had never come to this town, never walked into the shelter….

"Lily-kit, it's okay. We're here."

"We" in this case was Patrick, Aggie, a very young-looking woman named Abigail who was handling the tech and an older Asian man they called Abraham, although she wasn't sure if that was his first name, last name or nickname. The FBI had come through, although she got the feeling that Abraham at least thought it was all a waste of time.

"Lily. Showtime."

She nodded, picked up the phone. "Hello?"

"You know."

The reporter was wearing a dark pink sweater that made her complexion look sallow. They should have put her in something with more blue. "Do you think that the person who stole the cheetah intends to keep it as a pet, the way the ocelot you rescued last year was?"

"Oh, I hope not." Lily had done her best wide-eyed expression at the camera. "Big cats aren't the same at all as these little fellows," and she had cuddled a small spotted cat on her lap. Jon had told her to pick a tabby,

but she knew what would push the Night Serpent's buttons. The temple cats were spotted, but not tabbies. She had specifically requested a Mau, an Egyptian breed. They had to bring one in from a breeder in New Hampshire. Had there been one closer... Had there been one closer, they would all be dead now. "No more than, oh, a fighter jet is the same as a Cessna two-seater. One's fun and dangerous if you're not careful— the other...well, I've never flown a fighter jet, but I can imagine there are a lot more ways you can kill yourself faster than in a little passenger plane."

Jon and Abraham had put together a script for her to follow when the Night Serpent called. But it didn't feel right in her mouth.

She could hear him breathing on the other end of the line. The sounds in the room around her hushed the moment she picked up the phone, faded into nothingness. "I know a lot of things," she said, instead of what the script in front of her suggested. "What do you need from me?"

"The key. I need to know how to turn the key. Everything is ready, but it has to be tonight. It's my last chance. You know how to make everything go right."

Selfish, she thought. *Always selfish. Why hadn't she seen that before?* Then: *Tonight. The new moon. She had been right.*

"Why should I help you? What's in it for me?"

There was silence, as though he had never considered the question before. She was off-script in oh so many ways, but the men in the room couldn't interrupt her, not without giving the game away. *She* was in control here. She was the one calling the shots, directing the action.

"She says…" The Night Serpent's voice faded out, then came back more strongly. He had a nice voice, if a little too…narrow for her taste. His vowels were thin, not rounded. Odd, the things you noticed.

"What does She say?" Lily put capitals into the word, the same way he had.

"She says you know. You know. You have to tell me! I can't stay here any longer. Tonight, it's my last chance. The last chance there will ever be. I have to get it right."

"I'll trade you," she said, finally going back on-script, to the palpable relief of the others in the room. "I'll tell you what I know…and you give me back what you took. *Unharmed.*"

There was a silence. "I need…"

"You won't," she said as persuasively as she could. He was not going to kill another beast. Not one more. "Not once I tell you what I know."

Another silence, the weight of his decision hanging over them.

"All right."

"Where are you? I'll need to show you… You have to have everything just right." It was a risk, but based on his use of a specific pattern and the elaborate preparations of his last hiding spot, Jon thought that he would respond well to the suggestion of a ceremony or set-dressing that needed to be done.

The Serpent gave her directions. She didn't know the area, somewhere out of town proper, but Abraham nodded as though it made perfect sense to him.

"Be there. An hour."

And then he hung up.

"Wasn't he supposed to say 'and come alone'?" Lily wondered, as much to break the grip the tension had on her as to actually wonder.

"He's too focused on himself, his own needs," Jon said as Abigail gave Abraham a thumbs-up, indicating whatever they were doing with the tech had worked.

"Selfish," Lily said, this time out loud. "He's always been selfish."

Her lover gave her an odd look, but continued, "Anyway, they only really say that on television shows. Real criminals know that only an idiot goes in alone, without backup."

"Ms. Malkin?" Abraham approached them. "If we're to be there on time, we need to get moving. You will drive your car. We will follow at a distance. Try to keep us in your rearview mirror at all times, but don't be too concerned if we disappear—we will have you on display at all times."

"Display?"

"We put a tracker in the vest and on your car," Jon said. "Just in case we get separated by traffic."

"Oh." She thought a moment. "You'll take it out again, after."

"We have to account for every bug and bite at the end of every mission," Abraham assured her with a perfectly straight face. He might have been kidding. She didn't think that he was.

The technician packed up her stuff, and Abraham and Jon went into a huddle off in the corner.

Aggie, who had been watching silently, came up and put a heavy hand on her shoulder. His other hand reached into his pocket and came out with what looked like a small cell phone.

"Take this."

She did, turning it over in her hands.

"If anything goes wrong, or even feels like it's going to go wrong, you just press this button here, the green one, and you'll have half a dozen very cranky cops attached to your hip, k? Don't you wait on those federal nitwits."

He didn't like this; his feelings were clear on his face and in his voice. But he was going to put on a good, confident show for her. She couldn't do anything less for him.

"I got it, Aggie. Let's do this thing." She tried to put a swagger into her voice that she wasn't feeling at all, and gave a twisted grin in return before the agents came back with a tangle of wires and microphones to attach to her, and Aggie stepped into the background.

Abraham had told her to park at the far end of the lot, away from the other cars and most of the lights. She pulled into a slot and turned off the engine, and an SUV with tinted windows came up beside her.

Five minutes later she had been surrounded by half a dozen federal agents, having her jacket taken off and the electronics that had been attached to her double- and triple-checked, and adjusting the fit of the bulletproof vest under her jacket. They didn't think he would shoot her, they assured her; it was standard operating proce-dure, sending anyone into a potentially dangerous situation. Plus, they still weren't sure what he had used on the guards.

"I really don't like this thing," she said, tugging at the confining weight of the vest.

"Leave it alone," Jon said as he elbowed aside the last tech and adjusted her shirt with almost impersonal hands, letting his fingers linger a bit longer than might be normal at her waist. His touch was loving, but his voice was, barely, all business. "Just forget it's there, go in and get him talking. All we need is for you to engage him, get him to tell us where he has the cat. We can't risk it getting loose once we have him."

Lily nodded. It could have been worse. A tiger, for example. But any big cat was dangerous, if injured, or hungry or frightened. And in the hands of a half-mad, untrained psychopath? It was a disaster waiting to happen. And she was walking right into the den, so to speak.

He couldn't fiddle any longer, and sighed, stepping away. "It would be simpler to just go in there and take him out. I could have gotten a sniper in position…"

"He's not worth a sniper," Lily said, echoing Abraham's decision. "And you need him alive."

She wasn't just talking about the bureau. Jon needed this guy, too. He needed to talk to him, study him. Add that information to how he worked. And, not incidentally, justify his decision to go through all of this to catch him. The feds didn't need to be involved in all this, the state and city police had made that very clear. But Special Agent Patrick had put his fingerprints all over the case, and now he had his own people running the show.

His reputation was on the line.

She had never been important to anyone before.

Yes, you have. And been discarded once you were no longer useful.

It was different now. Jon Patrick was ambitious, but not a user. He would not abandon her. She had to believe that, or she'd never be able to walk in there.

"Piece of cake, right?" She gave him what she hoped was a reassuring smile, picked up her purse, and walked away from him and into the restaurant.

A well-dressed and very handsome young man met her the moment she walked in the door. "Good afternoon. Do you have a reservation?"

"I'm…supposed to meet someone at the bar."

"Of course. This way, please."

It was a nice place. Out of the way, but pretty, and the air smelled of—she sniffed the air, lifting her chin slightly as she did so—it smelled of steak, and fresh herbs, and the tang of wine and spirits.

She suddenly, badly, wanted a drink.

"Can I help you?" the bartender asked. He was also very handsome, if not so well dressed.

"Ginger ale, please?"

The one thing she wasn't going to have was alcohol. Not until they had this guy, and she was home, and she decided right then and there that as soon as this was all done and settled, she was going to go down to the shelter and adopt a kitten. A gray one. Or maybe one of the tigers.

She felt the cool plastic of the receiver hidden in her collar. They could hear her, and she could hear Jon if he flipped a toggle or some high-tech variation. The weight of the vest was like a tether to the earth, convincing her that this wasn't all simply some strange hallucination.

She reached into her pocket and felt the cell phone Aggie had given her.

She left it in her pocket. She wouldn't need it. Everything was going to be fine.

Her ginger ale came and she paid for it, idly twirling the straw to make the ice sink and then rise up again. Was she supposed to ask if there was a reservation under her name? Or maybe Serpent, table for two?

Or would it be more accurate to say it was a table for four?

"Lily Malkin."

She turned at the voice, and was greeted by a pleasantly bland young man with an open, friendly expression on his face. She started to open her mouth to say that yes, she was Lily, when the gentle blue eyes shaded dark, narrowed, his entire face becoming harder, more predatory.

The man from the shadows.

The man who had haunted her un-dreams.

Her lover.

Her killer.

"Lily." Jon's voice in her ear. "Lily, is it him? Give us some info!"

The man in front of her raised his hand, drawing her attention away from the facial overlay. Something dangled from his fingers, a dull clay-red and ugly and—

Lily swayed, trapped by the amulet in his hand. Her gaze narrowed, and her vision grayed to black.

"Lily!" Jon's voice in her ear, unheard. "Lily, talk to me!"

Chapter 17

Lily opened her eyes to a gray haze and aching muscles. She lay very still and tried to remember. Walking into the restaurant, ordering a drink. A man, approaching her. And then…nothing.

As her vision cleared, she realized that she was lying on her back, staring up at a featureless gray ceiling. No, not quite featureless. It had a texture to it that was almost familiar….

Concrete. The ceiling was made of concrete?

She turned her head to the right, and noted that the wall was made of concrete as well. No windows. No lights, except one dim lightbulb hung high up on the ceiling.

The room was, in fact, almost pitch-black. But she could see. Not quite as clear as day, but well enough.

"Your pupils are dilated again," she said. "You're using whatever light is available, like a cat...." Like a cat. Her eyes, dilating. Her fingers, flexing as though she was kneading, displaying claws. Her ears, hearing things she could not possibly hear. *I'm losing my mind....*

She almost convinced herself that she imagined the noise that followed her vocalizing. Her body froze in place, apprehension crawling all over her skin. There was another, similar noise, and Lily moved her head slowly, slowly on the cold—concrete again—floor, forcing herself to look to the left.

One look, and she sprang backward, sliding to her right—or she tried to, until the cold metal cuff around her wrist reached the end of the chain that was bolted to the floor, halting her progress.

What the hell?

The black-rimmed eyes of the great cat lying next to her watched her curiously, as though wondering what strange thing the hairless kitten would do next.

She was chained to the floor. She was—her brain starting to kick in slowly—stripped down to her underwear and bra, and chained to the floor of a windowless room. Made of concrete. *Cold* concrete. Next to a very large, very-much-not-a-moggy feline.

It blinked, the pale green eyes alert, but the pose unthreatening. A long, narrow tail flicked once, thumping down on the floor, but otherwise the cat didn't move from its side-sprawled pose next to her.

Literally—even after her attempted bolt, there was barely a foot between the two of them. The cat was grayed out in the non-light, but she could see well enough to tell that it was not quite as long, paw to ears, as she was tall, with lean muscle and a sleek build to go with that lazy tail. A surprisingly small, almost triangular head. Huge paws, with claws that would glint under a desert sun.

And it, unlike herself, was not chained or tied to anything.

"Oh God." Lily forced herself to start breathing again, and slowly blinked her eyes at it, the way she would a cat in the shelter she was trying to reassure. She had no idea if the gesture would work with a great cat.

It made that noise again. Not a purr, or a meow, or a roar. More like a chirp, like you would expect to hear from something the size of a groundhog, not a big cat. Almost as though…it was saying hello.

It seemed rude not to respond.

"Kurr, kurr," she ventured, hoping she wasn't actually saying, "Hello, come eat me while I'm chained up here and you're not."

It chirruped at her again, still watching with deceptive laziness, its eyes closing and opening slowly the same way hers had. A cheetah, her memory told her. The great hunting cat of the desert. The royal cat of the pharaohs.

The cheetah from the zoo. They had been right. Fat lot of good it did them now.

"You deserve better than this, swift one," she told it.

A grinding noise drew both their attention: a door was opening in the far wall. Light from outside came in, making Lily squint in pain.

"You brought others with you," he said in accusation. "You were wearing police gear. A wire."

The Night Serpent; backlit, she couldn't see his face. A haze surrounded him, making it difficult to focus. She didn't need to. She had known his face once better than she knew her own. Dark, handsome. Like Jon. But nothing like him.

"You didn't say to come alone." A joke, she wasn't sure how she managed it.

The foot that hit her ribs was a shock, and the cat growled but didn't move.

"You can eat him if you want," she said to the cat, refusing to let the man see her in pain. She didn't know where these wisecracks were coming from; it wasn't like her to mouth off. But it wasn't like her to be stalked by a lunatic, to become an FBI-approved piece of bait, to be drugged and stripped and chained to a *floor,* either. She was, she discovered, royally *pissed.* She glared up at her captor. "Or was that what he was supposed to do to me? Eat me?" How hungry did a cheetah have to be to make human flesh smell good?

He shrugged, less indifferent than refusing responsibility. "If the beast harms you, it is Her will."

A voice came out of her throat, her jaws moving, but not her words. "She cast me off long ago. Your doing."

A blade, a dark shadow, a searing cold pain in her side... Nothing compared to the pain of Her eyes turning away, refusing her....

Lily forced the memory down. She could not afford this, not now. Whatever was happening, she had to keep her mind clear. No confusion, no dizziness, no anything other than logical, rational thinking.

He came forward, allowing her night vision to see

him more clearly, but the haze remained. It wasn't a trick of the light, but rather her vision. The flesh was ordinary: a man of regular build, shaggy blond hair and mild features. Underneath, or over: the man she remembered in her nightmares. The face she saw outside the hospital, then again in the restaurant. The man from her past, her very first past. Had he been there in the others, too? The times between, where nothing had gone right, dooming her to repeat, over and over again…

"She cast us both off," he said. "Promised us everything, and delivered nothing. The power you gave me, it should have taken me to the next level, given me the abilities I craved, the abilities *you* have."

"You deserved nothing!"

His leg swung out again, crashing into her ribs. "All I needed was to turn the key in the lock you provided. All power and glory would have been mine then, with Her power at my disposal. But the key would not turn!"

The pain allowed the memories to sweep back over her, filling the spaces in her brain. "And they found you," she gasped, glaring at him. "Found what you had done. And you were judged…and found wanting."

"They stripped me of my status. Cast me out, cast me from power."

"They didn't kill you. A mercy you didn't show to me."

It was insane. Lily knew it, even as the words came out of her mouth. Talking to this man as if they were entirely different people.

She was Lily Malkin, damn it. She was an American.

She lived in the twenty-first century. She was a bank teller, for God's sake! She was not an ancient Egyptian priestess of some cat-headed god she didn't even believe in. And he was not an Egyptian high-caste noble with a thirst for power that overrode all other considerations and morals. It was impossible.

She would not accept it. She would *not*.

"You will tell me what I need to do. This time the key will turn, and I will be able to call forth the powers of the underworld. Be as one with the gods."

Real or unreal, both bank teller and priestess spoke with one unified voice: "You're insane."

He smiled at her. "Yes. Of course I am."

Lily blinked. *Oh.*

He spoke a word that resonated of command, and the cat rose to its feet slowly, almost as though moving against its will. "You see, it would love to attack me. It would love to rend me apart. And yet it cannot. I spent the years since awakening attaining the charm that protects me from claws and teeth." He touched his chest, and she saw a thin silver chain around his neck, dropping down below the collar of his shirt. The same thing he had used to—distract? Hypnotize? *Control* her, back in the bar. "She hungers for worship, in this cold world…but Her beasts do not trust me."

"Imagine that," Lily said dryly. He bent and tugged on the chain at her wrist. It came free from the floor with a flicker of sparks, and Lily tensed, wondering if she could rush him, knock him over….

Her ribs twinged where he had kicked her, and she relaxed her muscles. Even if she could take him by surprise, all he had to do was release the control he had over the cheetah, and she'd have about as much chance as a wounded gazelle of escaping. And where would she go, half-naked and shoeless? She didn't even know where they were, or how long…

Jon. How long had she been missing? Why hadn't he found her yet? Damn it, what use was backup if they didn't back you up?

Lily eyed the chain that now rested in his grip. "I have no idea what the key is, or how to turn it. She lied to you. She will not give you anything." The gods did not share, willingly or otherwise.

"She never lies. You know how to make Her lock turn. You just don't remember that you know. Yet. Get up." He yanked on the chain, and she had no choice but to obey.

They made an odd little parade: the cheetah walking ahead of them, tail slung low, ears flicking first forward then back as it led the way along the narrow hallway, then the Night Serpent, looking like a refugee from the suburbs in his khakis and button-down shirt, leading a half-naked woman by the arm—by means of a foot-long metal chain.

She was cold. Wherever they were, there wasn't much by way of heating. The floor was smooth and cool under the soles of her feet, and goose bumps were rising on her arms and legs.

Jon. Agent Patrick. Where the hell are you?

There was no answer. Fine. She was on her own. She always had been, really.

Inside, in some deep shadowy recess of her soul, something stirred and stretched, restless.

* * *

"Damn it, what do you mean you can't get a signal?"

Jon was ready to rip some hair out. His own, another's, he didn't much care. The moment Lily had walked into that damn restaurant the entire plan had gone to hell and it kept getting worse.

"Tell me again how a woman disappears from a restaurant with only thee exits, all of which were *supposed* to be watched by trained officers? Tell me again how the newest equipment we have can't track the woman who disappeared from that supposedly secured and observed location? And tell me—"

"Sir, if you would calm down…"

"Don't sir me. Just get me a signal."

He stalked off, leaving the small bustle behind as he stood under a tree, looking up at the sparse brown leaves without seeing them.

Nobody had taken this seriously enough. Not even him. Oh, he had taken the Night Serpent seriously enough—another data point for his charts, another example to build his theories around…another step up the agency ladder. Another career milestone.

But not as a threat. He hadn't considered the man enough of a threat. Not a deadly one. Not one he, in his ego, couldn't counter, just by being smarter, better prepared. His ego had put Lily in this situation. His arrogance had put her directly in the worst possible situation.

He turned away from the others and slammed his hand into the side of the tree. The pain didn't help.

Where are you, Lily? Help me find you….

* * *

They walked up a flight of stairs, and the floor changed from concrete to rough carpeting, like you might find in a low-end office building. A fire door swung open under the Serpent's hand, and Lily walked through into another room. This one was larger, with a skylight that let in faint sunlight.

Morning. She had been in that room overnight. The good guys weren't coming.

There was an arch against the far wall, made out of what looked like foam plastic, spray painted black, just like his last one. It was probably twice as tall as she was, and wide enough that she could have walked through it with her arms outstretched—assuming that she was then willing to walk into the wall it was leaning against. Directly in front of the arch was a large step, maybe five feet long, and draped in a black cloth.

Lily felt her gorge rise. It was the storefront all over again, only on a larger scale. And instead of seven house cats, he had one big cat to sacrifice. And he would make her watch, she had no doubt about that. And then she would follow, if—when—that didn't work. Would his…whatever he had that kept the cat obedient, would it have worked on more than one? She didn't think so. It was almost a shame he didn't take the pair, then.

"Beast. Sit. There."

The cat walked to the step and dropped his haunches, curling his paws under him and watching the man with an unblinking gaze.

"And you. Must I rechain you, or will you behave?"

"What am I going to do, make a break for it?" She looked down at herself, then back at him.

"Good. You have nothing to gain from fighting me. And you would lose. Again."

Lily sank against the wall, as far from the arch as she could get, drew her knees up and wrapped her arms around them. She was alone. She had no wires. No bulletproof vest. No cell phone with panic button. No… She made a noise that could have been a cry or a snort of laughter. No pants.

The Night Serpent was drawing a circle on the floor with red chalk. There were sigils along the circle. Seven of them. Something in Lily's memory—no, not her memory, that *other* memory—stirred, recognizing it, but she refused to allow it to rise into awareness. It didn't matter. None of it mattered. And even if it mattered, what could she do? The spark that had allowed her to talk back to the Night Serpent had gone as quickly as it appeared, leaving her cold and empty.

She had failed. Whatever madness the madman wanted, he would get.

The circle completed around the steps, he stood on one of the sigils—*Ren,* her other-memory told her. *Name.*

Sekhem. Energy of the dead.

Ab. Mother's heart.

Akh. The immortal aspect.

Ba. Personality.

Ka. Life force.

Sheut. Soul-shadow.

The seven sigils. The seven cats. The seven parts of

the human soul. *Sekhu. The physical remains. The Serpent himself.*

What was he doing?

Another memory crawled upward. Doors. Great heavy sliding doors, sealed with the touch of the Protectress, the fierce Lady of Flame, the goddess Bast. *Bastet. Lady Mother.*

The seven parts of the human soul. The parts of death. The doors to the underworld. Turn a key. Open a door. The words he had spoken rattled around in her head, fluttered delicate wings in her brain.

He wanted to open the doors to the underworld, to travel the paths of the dead. He was looking to reclaim the life that those shortsighted, hidebound fools had taken from him. A way to go back and exact revenge.

Impossible. She raised her gaze to the ceiling, as though expecting something to appear. Wasn't it?

He did not think so. He thought it was possible. The prickling of her skin told her that she—some part of her—thought it was, too.

The cat stirred, restless, clearly not wanting to remain passive. The Serpent—she could think of him no other way now, clearly seeing in his movements the relentless, almost hypnotic movements of a cobra— touched his amulet, and the cat stilled. The light glinted on his knife. Another life, another glorious, innocent life, sacrificed to his ego. His hunger.

"I'm sorry, beautiful one," she said to the cat, barely a whisper, but she saw the ears flicker toward her, and knew that it was listening. "You really do deserve better than this."

You cannot allow this.
You cannot allow this.
You cannot...
I know! she shot back, furious.

The voice, startled, left her alone.

The Serpent raised his knife, as though showing it to others in the room, and started to chant. A part of Lily recognized the words, but she let them wash over her, becoming background noise. It wasn't important. What was important was...

What? What was she supposed to do?

Stop him!

It wasn't rational. It wasn't smart. It was pretty much doomed to failure. And yet, without warning, a hundred and thirty pounds of incensed female slammed into a hundred ninety pounds of muscled male.

Surprise was in her favor. Entirely focused on the ceremony, his arrogance allowed him to ignore her once she agreed to stay still.

But that surprise fled, and once he recovered from the stagger, a powerful backhand across her jaw sent Lily halfway across the room.

"Bitch! I would have rewarded you, made you as powerful as you once were, but again you defy me!"

Instinct made her reach out when she saw his hand coming at her. Her fingers closed around something even as she was moving backward.

It was a toss-up who was more surprised: Lily or the Serpent, when she looked down at her hand and—despite vision dizzy from another probable concussion—saw the chain from around his neck wrapped in her fingers.

The amulet, freed, had slid off the chain and landed on the floor between them with a hard clunk. It laid there, a seven-sided disk made of bronze about the size of her palm, with a triangle-shaped hole cut in the middle. There were small red stones set in it, and some sort of writing between the stones.

The Serpent lunged for it at the same moment Lily shoved herself across the floor, trying to get to it first. The amulet was the secret. If he didn't have it, he couldn't control the great cat. Or the smaller ones. His power—his danger—lay in possessing the amulet.

He reached it first.

Desperate, Lily scooted backward, and, instead of trying to attack him again, flung open the door behind her.

"Go!" she screamed, loud and harsh enough to make the Serpent pause, his hand just over the amulet, for an instant.

In that instant, the cheetah leaped off the step and disappeared out the door.

"No!" he cried, scooping up the amulet and racing after it. Lily rolled over onto her side, ignoring the crackling of her ribs, and closed her eyes. *All right. All right.*

In that instant, she could *feel* the great cat moving through the halls, heading unerringly for an open window at the end. Muscles flexing for the first time in days, blood streaming, eyes alert. The human was behind, but far enough that the nasty-smelling metal could not affect it. They were on the first floor, and the air between the cat's whiskers was testing the distance, the width of a half-open window, the environment outside the window even as its muscles were bunching to leap, land and escape.

Gone.

The rush of power hummed in her veins, and Lily smiled.

She kept smiling even as the Serpent slammed back into the room, grabbing her by the arm and hauling her painfully to her feet. She kept smiling even when he slapped her hard across the face with the hand holding the amulet, the metal cutting her cheek open.

She kept smiling even as he hauled her across the room and shoved her down to her knees on the step.

"She thought to trick me. She thought to cheat me again! But not this time. No, not this time. She outwitted herself. I know what the key is. The true key. The reason I failed last time, more fool me. It is not the beasts whose blood binds the way, but Hers. And you are Her, here and now. *You* are the key." He fumbled for the knife with his free hand.

It is time, my daughter. You are almost done. Come home now to me.

The priestess smiled, and opened her eyes. Everything was brighter, sharper, the colors muted but the details clear, intense. When he raised the knife over her head, the itch in her fingertips became a burn. When the knife came down, she blocked it with her arm, her claws raking along his skin. The smell of blood rising from the scratches she left behind made her smile into a teeth-baring grin, her lips pulled back to better taste it in the air.

She twisted under his next blow, her spine moving,

more supple than anything human could manage. All hesitation, all distance was gone, and she lived in the moment, felt herself caught up in the greater pattern. She was *connected.* She landed a blow to his face, claws scoring him under his nose, up the side of his face.

"Bitch." The Serpent spat at her, a gob of saliva landing on her forearm. She could swear she heard it sizzle, even as he yanked her by the hair, bringing her face onto the floor. She felt the knife hiss against her skin, down the line of her spine, and she smelled the familiar tang of her own blood as it came to the surface. His hand scraped along the cut, pulling the wound open until she screamed from the pain, his hand dipping *into* the wound. Pain moved into agony, and she convulsed, arms and legs flailing as though in a fit.

Just as she thought she might—*must*—pass out from the intensity, he dropped her, moving across the room. He was muttering something under his breath, getting louder as he strode to the makeshift archway. The words swam in her ears: she thought she should understand them, but they refused to make sense. His intent, however, was unmistakable.

No! the voice—her voice—cried. *It must not be allowed!*

She rolled onto her side, stretching out as though she could reach him by force of will alone. Her fingers, the small, sharp claws curling out from under the tips, flexed, and then fell to her sides as her strength failed her.

I am not enough. Not then. Not now.

He was shouting now, flicking his fingers onto the

archway—no, through the archway. The words were not in English, but she understood every one.

"If you will not accept the key, then let the lock be broken! If you will not accept the key, then let the lock be broken." Again, his voice shaking with the force of his words. "If you will not accept the key, then let the lock be broken! With this once-sanctified blood, let the lock be broken, and the gates be opened!" He flicked his fingers again, scattering blood—her blood—into the space under the archway. "Open the secrets of the underworld to me! I will walk forever, and know death never again! Never again, do you hear!"

"You fool," she whispered. "You horrible fool."

He flicked blood again, a third time. And the archway shimmered, a terrible, awe-ful blackness taking form…

Chapter 18

The archway might only have been foam. The wall behind it might have been solid as stone could get. But that was in *this* world, and the Night Serpent's actions had broken the Gate between *this* world and *that* one. Sprawled prone across the step and bleeding heavily, Lily could only turn her head and watch as the black swirled and emerged from the archway, the wall-that-had-been now an abyss of flickering black sparks rising from a darker black pit.

She was Lily. She was herself. But the priestess's memories stayed with her, surging through her, telling her what to do.

She slid backward, her body screaming protest, until she was off the step, half hidden behind it. The Serpent stood in front of the archway, his arms spread as though welcoming a bride, or a long-lost friend.

Fool, she thought, the back of her neck hackling. *Fool.* It was as much a hiss as a thought. The muscles in her legs and arms twitched to be away, to leap and race down the hallway, away from what was coming, but she could barely move beyond where she had landed. Her spine twitched, as though a tail had just swished in agitation behind her.

This is… Bad. So very very bad. The priestess's memories were telling her that, but Lily knew it for truth on her own. Whatever was on the other side of that Gate, she did not want to be around for its arrival.

The sparks grew, coming closer, and her nose scrunched at the horrible smell that reached it: dank and dry at the same time musty and sharp. Underlying it all, bitterness. It was familiar, the way too many things recently had been familiar.

"Goddess, no, Mother, protect me!" she whispered, her eyes going wide and dark as the room filled with an ominous light. *Things* were visible now through the archway: large, misshapen *things,* moving with a heavy shuffle that did not hide the sense of menace rising from them.

The Serpent shuddered, his entire body quivering under the force of their approach, but he held steady. No one could ever have said that he was not brave. But he had never been privy to the workings of the temple, to the doings outside of the public eye. He was not a priest, despite the amulet he held. The amulet that would do nothing to protect him against what was coming.

I cannot allow this, Lily thought. *I cannot allow this to happen.* She owed him nothing; she would have been pleased to let the walkers of the underworld teach him what it meant to truly walk the Paths of the Dead. But it would not end there. The woman-she-had-been knew that, knew that the way she knew everything else. The Gate was locked for a reason. Locked, and left closed for all these ages…

Dizziness assaulted her, the blood loss and stress conspiring to make her head swim. Visions assaulted her: the long deserts of home, the cool marble, the sun and shimmer of light on the river followed in an endless stream of other lives. The cold of a forest where no light broke through. A wooden house filled with the emptiness of loneliness and age. A long gilded hallway, empty but for the ghosts of couples dancing. More, until the last, of standing at the doorway of the shelter. Terrified, determined and holding tight against the wave of uncertain emotion. She had thought it was internal, her own failures battering against her.

Now, in this instant, she knew it for what it had been: the welcome of the hundred-plus souls within, their small sparks recognizing what had been so deeply hidden within her.

All this, filtering through her like water into limestone, leaving behind the grit and coming out cleansed and whole. Complete.

She was the priestess. The priestess was Lily.

Eight times she had failed. Not from any flaw within her, save the one she allowed others to place there. Doubt. She had not trusted herself.

The first figure stepped across the sill of the arch. Another followed, hard on its heels.

Lady of Fire, Guardian of the Hearth, allow me to serve...

The words of the morning prayer rose to Lily's lips, even as she forced her body up into some sort of crouching position. The pain faded, and she felt her body begin to...

Change.

"Naaaaaaaah!" The sound was torn from her throat in a long scream: a mad, wild sound. Ignoring the pain of her ripped and bleeding body, she threw herself forward, stretching into the air, her arms forward, legs back, head tucked as she went past the Serpent, past the misshapen figure, to the archway itself. Her paws flexed, huge curved claws extending to swipe hard across the face of the archway, knocking several of the shambling figures a few steps back into the swirling abyss.

Another swipe, and the misshapen things retreated farther. They moaned, hungry for the light and life held in front of them, and Lily snarled, a harsh-edged, angry warning. She had no desire to destroy them—it was not their fault the door had opened—but she would not allow them to leave the underworld, either. Dead was dead, and must not move among the living again. The worst zombie movie ever barely touched on the horrors that would follow, not only for the living but also for the dead whose *ka,* spirit, would be disturbed, unable to find peace while their bodies walked....

Go sleep, she told them, her voice a harsh snarl.

Return to your crypts and fade into the shadows so your souls may be reborn without burdens, without pain. Sleep, sleep forevermore.

The words failed to halt them, and the figures started to shuffle forward again, drawn inexorably toward the light and warmth of the living world.

She raised a paw to stop them, part of her dimly aware that her hand was glowing with a faint blue light. Or was it just the way her skin looked against the red-black light coming from the Gate?

Stop, she snarled. *Go back. I command you.* Her body lurched forward, the adrenaline that supported her initial lunge having long since drained away. One of the figures lurched as though a mirror image. Its face was misshapen, eye sockets torn, nose ripped and decaying. It looked at her, not with hatred, but pleading.

Stop, she said again, this time more softly. *This place is not for you.*

The blue light met the red-black, and a darker green appeared, pulsing like a heart, in and out, fast at first then slowing until it stilled. The nearest figure tried to fight her off, grabbing at her arm as though to tear it off, but the green barred it from her.

Close, she told the Gate. *Seal.* Her voice came through firm and in command, the wind blowing from a faraway land. *The Lady of Flame commands it.*

"No!" A hand grabbed at her, pulling her backward, knocking her off her feet. The green light pulsed once again, spreading to cover the entire surface of the archway, sealing it once again.

"No!"

If she had thought the Night Serpent insane before, he was maddened now, his jaw hanging open, bubbles of froth flowing over the corner of his narrow lips. His eyes had gone shallow, flicking back and forth like the movement of the creature whose name he had claimed, quicksilver and dangerous. He hissed, his jaw dropping even wider, and lunged as though to sink his fangs into her flesh.

She reacted to him not as woman to man, but cat to snake, hissing and lashing out with teeth and claws, slashing at his face and forearms, looking to drop him into the dust and rend his poisonous flesh. She struck hard, but her claws were not enough to finish the job, and he knocked her aside once again, looming over her.

The blue glow around her seemed to hesitate, then condensed into a darker glow, closer to her skin. Lily closed her eyes, then, despite the blood still seeping from the gaping wound in her back, somehow found the strength to spring at him again, her teeth trying to find his jugular and rip it out.

He fought her off, a heavy backhand landing across her face. "Bitch. Traitorous bitch! I would have—"

"Killed me. Again." She spat blood, struggling as he tried to wrap his hands around her own neck. A squirm, her spine twisting until she landed on all fours, inches away. But the wall was to her back, and he was between her and the only door.

She was going to die. Again.

"You wanted power, but always someone else's, taken from them. Fool!" She laughed, bitterly amused despite the blood dripping from her mouth and the feel of teeth loosened in her mouth. "You always…were…a fool. And me, for trusting you. But not this time. Not this time… I stopped you. *I. Stopped. You.*"

She might die. She probably would die. It was all right: she had done what she came back to do. Finally.

Distantly, she heard a commotion outside, far away, but getting closer, coming toward them. The Serpent reared back, readying for a final blow.

Lily should have ducked, should have tried to run. All she could do was stare up into his eyes: dark burning pits of desert fire, wrapped around with the sound of sand blowing and the low muttering growl of a crocodile on the sun-warmed mud of the Nile. She felt herself start to sway in rhythm to his own lithe movements, even as she told herself to blink, to look away.

A hissing cough broke into the sounds in her head, and vision flashed away from her. When it returned, her line of sight was lower to the ground, moving rapidly as things came into focus and then faded again. The look of things was wrong: too flat, too gray and blue. The sun was not bright or warm enough for comfort, and the air tasted of harsh metal, not the warm comfort of blood and flesh.

Cat, she thought, barely holding on to any sense of herself under the onslaught, and felt its agreement. *Beautiful one. Run.* Agreement again, but not the way she intended. It wasn't running away. It was coming toward her. And it wasn't, it proudly informed her, coming alone.

Her mate was with him.

Lily barely had time to process that before the door

from the hallway crashed open. The Serpent went down
to one knee, turning and with one arm crushing Lily to
him, the other hand grabbing his knife off the floor. Her
vision returned to her with a snap, hard enough to make
her dizzy—or was that the blood loss? She wasn't sure
anymore. Everything was becoming fuzzy, grayed out
around the edges.

Then the shining tip of the Serpent's knife nicked
the delicate skin under her chin, sliding to rest directly
over her pulse, and her concentration returned with a
hard crunch.

Suddenly, she wasn't ready to die.

"Stop!"

The voice was painfully, wonderfully familiar. Lily
didn't have to look up to know who it was; she did it
merely to satisfy the desire to see him again. Jon: his
gun held in both hands, his body turned sideways like
some hero on a television show. Beautiful man. He was
dressed in black and gray, a windbreaker over a bulletproof vest like the one they had given her, and the
cheetah was a molten golden and black statue at his
side.

Her gaze flicked from the green-eyed stare of the cat
up to the stark cold lines of the gun, and stayed there. Her
bloody claws flexed, and she knew that Jon saw them.
She *meant* for him to see them. But the gun never
wavered.

He saw me. He saw me, and understood, and came,
the cat told her. *Good mate.*

Very, she told it back.

"I'll kill her," the Serpent said, his voice cold and

cool, as though he had never lost his temper in his entire
life. In all his lives. "I will kill her and you will have lost."

"You think that you can beat a bullet, be my guest,"
Jon said in a voice just as cold and cool. Lily felt the
knife dig in a little more, and raised her eyes from the
gun to look into her mate's face.

He wasn't bluffing.

She had been right about Jon T. Patrick, and she had
been completely wrong. Agent Patrick was dedicated
to his job, and the demanding mistress named Justice.
She respected that about him. She might even love that
about him. He was also a man who had been able to take
a leap of faith, no matter how improbable: to see the
glimmer of a cheetah's body in the grass, and know
what it meant. To follow it. To trust it.

But her body hurt too much to follow that thought
any further. Held upright only by the Serpent's grip on
her throat, every cell of her body was screamingly
aware of what it had been through. If he let go, even for
an instant, she would collapse in on herself, and
possibly never come back. Her fingers itched horribly,
and she risked a look down to see the claws slowly
retract back into her fingertips, leaving behind blood-
smeared tips over unbroken skin. Whatever gifts she
had been given, they were leaving her.

It was all right. She had done what she needed to do.
The Gate was closed. Jon could shoot this bastard and
it would all be over. Nine lives, game over. No replay
this time, not for either of them.

She wasn't ready to die, but who ever was? She only
hoped that Anubis' judgment would be gentle this time.

Lily's gaze dropped again, resting on the blunt lines of the cheetah's muzzle. Green eyes stared into hers, the lids closing once, slowly. A sleepy wink, the sort one cat gave another to indicate that all was well, he wasn't a threat, there was peace between them.

"Thank you," she said to the cat. For coming back. For not killing her in that storeroom, despite what must have been overwhelming instinct. For being a reminder of the beauty she had once known.

Sister-two-foot. This is not over yet.

Mrrraaai she told it, and felt the cat's amusement at her kitten-acceptance.

The Serpent jabbed her with the knife, stopping the conversation and drawing blood from her throat to match the red clotting in the rims of her nostrils and down the line of her back.

There was blood inside her throat, too, and her ribs made breathing difficult. She was aware of all this now, merely mortal again. She was dying. But that was all right. The Gate waited, and there would be peace on the other side. She hoped.

She braced herself for one last lunge, willing her fingers to work, even without the gift of claws. If she could distract him, Jon could finish the job. The Serpent must not escape. His punishment must be final this time.

Before she could do anything, a noise vibrated up through the soles of her feet, up into her bones, a strange guttural humming. She felt it, and saw the great cat's long tail twitch once, a hard *thwack* against the air. Those were the only warnings, and they happened so quickly the Serpent didn't have a chance to react before that long line of lean muscle was airborne.

But the cat wasn't aiming for the Serpent. A jaw that might have clamped down on him and done damage, claws that might have shredded skin from bones, none of those made contact. Instead, that jaw closed firmly but gently on Lily's shoulder, while the cat's own shoulder knocked into her with a solid thunk.

All three went sprawling to the floor. The cheetah twisted in midair, a seemingly impossible move, to land *under* Lily rather than on top of her, forcing her to land on her side rather than her injured back.

It still hurt like hell, but she managed not to pass out. The Serpent was down on his knees in front of her, and she wanted oh so badly to kick him between the legs, hard. If she could just move her leg. Or even her arm. She'd be willing to hit him, too. All of her rage came back and spilled over, fueled by the rumbling breath of the cat beneath her. Selfish, stupid…he had opened the Gate, all for his own selfish desires and wants, like a spoiled five-year-old. Did he not understand that the dead needed to stay dead? That allowing the Gate to open…

Disease. At the very least. Imbalance.

The Serpent looked across at her, and she shivered. His eyes were no longer blue and kind, or even black and intense; now they were flat and inhuman looking. Not even a serpent's eyes, but dull as a river stone. A trickle of blood came from his left nostril, matching the one at the corner of his mouth. She tasted her own blood pooling in her mouth, and felt no sympathy.

"I…I would have…" he rasped, staring at her as if she still held some kind of answer. She had no answers to give him, and he seemed to realize that, because he started to get to his feet, the knife still clutched in his hand.

"Stay down!" Jon commanded. Who was he talking to? Lily could hear more noises from the hallway—someone else was coming? Help, or did the Serpent have allies? She struggled to back away, get to her own feet and out of his reach, only to have the heavy, meat-sweet breath of the cheetah hit her cheek. He had stretched just enough so that the heavy triangular head rested against her cheek, as though it were trying to scent-mark her, and the weight pressed her down to the ground.

Down. Stay down. Do as the mate says.

Not words now, but a sense of insistence, of concern, of worry that the small one would not be wise, would get hurt.

All right, she thought. *All right.* She didn't have the strength to do anything else anyway.

"Down, I said!" Jon sounded pissed off. "Robert Bergman, you are under arrest for the kidnapping and unlawful imprisonment of Lily Malkin, among other bad moves. Lie on the floor with your hands over your head. Now!"

Instead, the Serpent closed his fist tighter around his knife and swung at Lily, aiming directly for her heart. A name from this time, this place, had no power over him. Whatever Jon had discovered could not be used to stop him.

The cat screamed, a sound that should not come

from a cheetah's throat, and Lily felt it as though it came from her own mouth, even as there was a harsh heavy noise, the sound of gunfire and an acrid smell like blood-warmed dust in her nose.

The Night Serpent hovered over her; a boogeyman slithered out from under the bed in the dark of night, the knife no longer glinting but covered in gore and blood. A matching blossom of red bloomed on the front of his shirt, and his throat was torn away, making his head loll to the side. The entire room crashed into silence that hung for one, two, three breaths….

Then he fell, the cheetah's bloody muzzle shoving Lily out of the way just before he would have landed on top of her. The room exploded into noise and action, men in dark blue and gray everywhere, filling every available space.

The Serpent lay on the floor next to her, his face slack, his pale blue eyes open and sightless. A lock of pale blond hair fell over his forehead, making him look absurdly young.

Is done, the cat said in satisfaction. *Judgment.*

Lily turned away, rested her face on the dense plush fur of the cat, and felt one hard, bitter tear fall from her eye.

She had no idea whom she was crying for.

"Ma'am? Ma'am? Ms. Malkin?" Abraham, the guy who had come up from D.C. to oversee the operation. He was in her face, and she batted at him, trying to make him go away.

"Don' like you."

He looked taken aback, then grinned. The grin looked strange on him, like he didn't do it very often. "Very few people do, Ms. Malkin."

They had given her something for the pain. It didn't make the pain go away, but she didn't give a damn about it anymore.

"You got him." She would not give him the benefit of a name. Not the one he'd worn here, not the one he'd had in their days together, not even the one that the media had given him. He would be nameless to her, forevermore. It was right. It was just.

"More like to say the cat did," Abraham said. "Damn cat—we can't figure what killed the guy, the bullet or the bite. That guy won't be hurting anyone again, though, not anymore."

"No. Not anymore," she agreed peaceably. Abraham had no idea. No idea at all.

Then the EMTs returned and bundled her into an ambulance, securing her in her stretcher so that she wouldn't bump or slide on the way to the hospital. It was a little like beings trapped on a roller coaster, she thought. There was a burst of conversation, someone arguing, and then they closed the doors and the ambulance pulled away, hands and voices still fussing around her. Even through the fussing, with her eyes closed, Lily knew that Jon was there, beside her in the narrow, crowded space.

"That was," he said, his voice still cool, "possibly the stupidest thing anyone has ever done. Ever."

Lily opened her eyes and looked at him, then raised one hand—a human hand, with human nails, not claws and pads—and touched the side of his face. It took too much effort, and exhausted her, just that one movement. The skin of his cheek was dry, prickly with beard growth. It was the most wonderful thing she had ever felt.

"Which part?" she asked.

He caught her hand with his own, holding her touch against his face. "Yes," he said, and his voice was warm all of a sudden. "Yes."

She smiled, feeling the texture of his skin and the weight of his gaze on her. Unblinking. Unflinching. He had seen. He might not know what he had seen, but he had seen. And he was here. He was still here. He hadn't thrown her away, hadn't walked away.

She had broken the cycle.

"I'm a heroine," she said to him, drowsy from the painkillers. "You gotta tell me. What does the T stand for?"

This time, he laughed. "Tiberius," he admitted. "My mom was a *Star Trek* fan, but my dad wouldn't let her name me James because he had an Uncle James he didn't like. I hate it."

"Jon Tiberius. Goddess, that's awful," she said dreamily. Then an EMT shoved Jon aside and leaned over her to adjust the flow of liquids into her veins. She closed her eyes and let the darkness take her.

It was all right. Jon T. would be there when she woke up.

Chapter 19

The air was cold, an arctic front swooping down and reclaiming the season. Lily stood on the tiny balcony of her condo and looked up at the sky. There were no clouds, and the stars were still and clear.

For the first time ever, the stars looked *right*.

The sliding door opened and closed behind her, and Jon came up behind her. He paused just before actually making contact, waiting for her to lean into him. When she did, he wrapped his arms around her, careful to avoid the bandages under her sweater, covering the cuts and scratches on her shoulders and arms. They were all from the Serpent's knife; the cat's claws never touched her, even as he was knocking her to the ground.

The cheetah had taken the brunt of the Serpent's knife in its side, even as it knocked her clear, allowing Jon an open shot at the man. One of the agents, risking his own life, had bundled the injured cat into the back of his car and driven it to the hospital himself, yelling at the emergency-room staff until someone got on the phone with the zoo, getting instructions over the line on how to sedate the cat and sew it up.

Lily had heard the story after, when it was funny, not terrifying. She suspected that the agent and the E.R. crew would all dine out on that story for months to come.

As though he knew what she was thinking, Jon told her, "The cat's gotten a clean bill of health, and will be picked up by his facility tomorrow morning."

She nodded. She knew that already, from the cat's humming contentment she could feel even now in her bones, even across town. She knew that connection would fade the way the rest of it, the memories and the scars, were already fading. But that awareness wouldn't go away, not unless she wanted it to.

She very much didn't want it to. Not now. Not that she knew what it was. What *she* was.

"I still can't believe he found you," she said. Cheetahs had been used as hunting animals back then, and even now, but they were sight hunters, not smell. The ability to find Jon, and bring him back, across an unfamiliar, probably terrifying city…

"It was a miracle," she said finally, not willing to

push it further. Not willing to say the word the cat had bandied about so carelessly. Not yet.

"It was something," Jon agreed. He still wasn't sure what, hadn't been able to say the words, but his training was to follow the evidence, and build theories on what he knew for a fact. And he knew for a fact that a cat had helped him save his lover.

And she knew that he knew for a fact that his lover had eyes that reflected light like that cat's. That cats adored her, spoke to her. That when they made love, sometimes he felt the prick of claws, gentle, on his skin.

"There's going to be holy hell to pay when I go back to D.C. Boss isn't going to be happy to have his fair-haired boy wandering away from home."

The shooting, in full sight of half a dozen Fibbies and local cops, was ruled—what phrase had they used?—righteous—and Special Agent Jon T. Patrick was, if not a hero, then a guy who done good.

She leaned her head back against his shoulder and looked up at the sky again. "Done good" had such a lovely sound to it. So did the idea of him transferring here. It wasn't D.C. He wasn't going to climb the ladder quite so fast. But if he was okay with it, she was more than okay with it. Anyway, that was why they put "federal" in FBI; he would travel, and then come home.

Home.

She closed her eyes, and breathed out a prayer. In the distance, she could feel the whisper of cats' thoughts as they moved through the night, intent on their small, secretive ways. They dreamed of tasty mice and grand schemes, of warm hearths and gentle hands. And deep inside them all, the soft and fierce presence of the goddess rested.

In Lily's heart, as well.

"Making a wish?" he asked, only half joking.

"Should I?" She used to wish for all sorts of things: a best friend, a lover, an end to her phobias and her nightmares. A place where she felt that she belonged.

"Nobody's ever going to believe any of this, you know," he said, going back to the discussion they had started over dinner. "The cat finding me, the way I found you… They're creating reasons that work for them, that make sense."

"What makes sense to you?" It was the first time she'd had the courage to ask him directly.

He chuckled, low in his throat like a purr. "Nothing. None of it makes any sense. But I have this theory I'm working on…."

"Of course you do."

His arms tightened around her, and he looked up at the sky as well, reciting, "Star light, star bright, I've got every damn thing I want tonight."

She giggled, the way he had intended her to.

"It's over?" he asked, solemn again. "Your spells, the attacks…?"

"It's over," she agreed, settling against him, feeling totally, completely secure in him, in herself. In them. And, quietly, she thought to herself, *Or maybe it's just begun.*

She thought that maybe it *was* time to go to the shelter, bring someone home.

And somewhere in the non-distance of time, she felt a vaguely feline, powerful purr of approval.

* * * * *

Don't miss Anna Leonard's
next Nocture coming in 2009!
And be sure to check out her Nocturne Bite at
www.eharlequin.com.

Turn the page for a sneak preview of
AFTERSHOCK, *a new anthology*
featuring New York Times *bestselling author*
Sharon Sala.

Available October 2008.

n●cturne™

Dramatic and sensual tales of paranormal romance.

Chapter 1

October
New York City

Nicole Masters was sitting cross-legged on her sofa while a cold autumn rain peppered the windows of her fourth-floor apartment. She was poking at the ice cream in her bowl and trying not to be in a mood.

Six weeks ago, a simple trip to her neighborhood pharmacy had turned into a nightmare. She'd walked into the middle of a robbery. She never even saw the man who shot her in the head and left her for dead. She'd survived, but some of her senses had not. She was dealing with short-term memory loss and a tendency to stagger. Even though she'd been told the problems were most likely temporary, she waged a daily battle with depression.

Her parents had been killed in a car wreck when she was twenty-one. And except for a few friends—and most recently her boyfriend, Dominic Tucci, who lived in the apartment right above hers, she was alone. Her doctor kept reminding her that she should be grateful to be alive, and on one level she knew he was right. But he wasn't living in her shoes.

If she'd been anywhere else but at that pharmacy when the robbery happened, she wouldn't have died twice on the way to the hospital. Instead of being grateful that she'd survived, she couldn't stop thinking of what she'd lost.

But that wasn't the end of her troubles. On top of everything else, something strange was happening inside her head. She'd begun to hear odd things: sounds, not voices—at least, she didn't think it was voices. It was more like the distant noise of rapids—a rush of wind and water inside her head that, when it came, blocked out everything around her. It didn't happen often, but when it did, it was frightening, and it was driving her crazy.

The blank moments, which is what she called them, even had a rhythm. First there came that sound, then a cold sweat, then panic with no reason. Part of her feared it was the beginning of an emotional breakdown. And part of her feared it wasn't—that it was going to turn out to be a permanent souvenir of her resurrection.

Frustrated with herself and the situation as it stood, she

upped the sound on the TV remote. But instead of *Wheel of Fortune,* an announcer broke in with a special bulletin.

"This just in. Police are on the scene of a kidnapping that occurred only hours ago at The Dakota. Molly Dane, the six-year-old daughter of one of Hollywood's blockbuster stars, Lyla Dane, was taken by force from the family apartment. At this time they have yet to receive a ransom demand. The housekeeper was seriously injured during the abduction, and is, at the present time, in surgery. Police are hoping to be able to talk to her once she regains consciousness. In the meantime, we are going now to a press conference with Lyla Dane."

Horrified, Nicole stilled as the cameras went live to where the actress was speaking before a bank of microphones. The shock and terror in Lyla Dane's voice were physically painful to watch. But even though Nicole kept upping the volume, the sound continued to fade.

Just when she was beginning to think something was wrong with her set, the broadcast suddenly switched from the Dane press conference to what appeared to be footage of the kidnapping, beginning with footage from inside the apartment.

When the front door suddenly flew back against the wall and four men rushed in, Nicole gasped. Horrified, she quickly realized that this must have been caught on a security camera inside the Dane apartment.

As Nicole continued to watch, a small Asian woman, who she guessed was the maid, rushed forward in an effort to keep them out. When one of the men hit her in the face with his gun, Nicole moaned. The violence was too reminiscent of what she'd lived through. Sick to her stomach, she fisted her hands against her belly, wishing it was over, but unable to tear her gaze away.

When the maid dropped to the carpet, the same man followed with a vicious kick to the little woman's midsection that lifted her off the floor.

"Oh, my God," Nicole said. When blood began to pool beneath the maid's head, she started to cry.

As the tape played on, the four men split up in different directions. The camera caught one running down a long marble hallway, then disappearing into a room. Moments later he reappeared, carrying a little girl, who Nicole assumed was Molly Dane. The child was wearing a pair of red pants and a white turtleneck sweater, and her hair was partially blocking her abductor's face as he carried her down the hall. She was kicking and screaming in his arms, and when he slapped her, it elicited an agonized scream that brought the other three running. Nicole watched in horror as one of them ran up and put his hand over Molly's face. Seconds later, she went limp.

One moment they were in the foyer, then they were gone.

Nicole jumped to her feet, then staggered drunkenly.

The bowl of ice cream she'd absentmindedly placed in her lap shattered at her feet, splattering glass and melting ice cream everywhere.

The picture on the screen abruptly switched from the kidnapping to what Nicole assumed was a rerun of Lyla Dane's plea for her daughter's safe return, but she was numb.

Before she could think what to do next, the doorbell rang. Startled by the unexpected sound, she shakily swiped at the tears and took a step forward. She didn't feel the glass shards piercing her feet until she took the second step. At that point, sharp pains shot through her foot. She gasped, then looked down in confusion. Her legs looked as if she'd been running through mud, and she was standing in broken glass and ice cream, while a thin ribbon of blood seeped out from beneath her toes.

"Oh, no," Nicole mumbled, then stifled a second moan of pain.

The doorbell rang again. She shivered, then clutched her head in confusion.

"Just a minute!" she yelled, then tried to sidestep the rest of the debris as she hobbled to the door.

When she looked through the peephole in the door, she didn't know whether to be relieved or regretful.

It was Dominic, and as usual, she was a mess.

Nicole smiled a little self-consciously as she opened the door to let him in. "I just don't know what's happening to me. I think I'm losing my mind."

"Hey, don't talk about my woman like that."

Nicole rode the surge of delight his words brought. "So I'm still your woman?"

Dominic lowered his head.

Their lips met.

The kiss proceeded.

Slowly.

Thoroughly.

* * * * *

Be sure to look for the AFTERSHOCK *anthology next month, as well as other exciting paranormal stories from Silhouette Nocturne. Available in October wherever books are sold.*

nocturne™

NEW YORK TIMES BESTSELLING AUTHOR

SHARON SALA

JANIS REAMES HUDSON
DEBRA COWAN

AFTERSHOCK

Three women are brought to the brink of death...
only to discover the aftershock of their trauma has
left them with unexpected and unwelcome gifts of
paranormal powers. Now each woman must learn to
accept her newfound abilities while fighting for life,
love and second chances....

Available October wherever books are sold.

www.eHarlequin.com
www.paranormalromanceblog.wordpress.com   SN61796

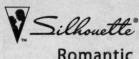

Romantic SUSPENSE

**Sparked by Danger,
Fueled by Passion.**

USA TODAY bestselling author

Merline Lovelace

Undercover Wife

CODENAME: DANGER

Secret agent Mike Callahan, code name Hawkeye,
objects when he's paired with sophisticated
Gillian Ridgeway on a dangerous spy mission
to Hong Kong. Gillian has secretly been in love
with him for years, but Hawk is an overprotective
man with a wounded past that threatens to
resurface. Now the two must put their lives—
and hearts—at risk for each other.

Available October wherever books are sold.

REQUEST YOUR FREE BOOKS!

2 FREE NOVELS PLUS 2 FREE GIFTS!

Silhouette®

nocturne™

Dramatic and Sensual Tales of Paranormal Romance.

YES! Please send me 2 FREE Silhouette® Nocturne™ novels and my 2 FREE gifts (gifts are worth about $10). After receiving them, if I don't wish to receive any more books, I can return the shipping statement marked "cancel." If I don't cancel, I will receive 4 brand-new novels every other month and be billed just $4.47 per book in the U.S. or $4.99 per book in Canada, plus 25¢ shipping and handling per book plus applicable taxes, if any*. That's a savings of about 15% off the cover price! I understand that accepting the 2 free books and gifts places me under no obligation to buy anything. I can always return a shipment and cancel at any time. Even if I never buy another book from Silhouette, the two free books and gifts are mine to keep forever.

238 SDN ELS4 338 SDN ELXG

Name _____ (PLEASE PRINT) _____

Address _____ Apt. # _____

City _____ State/Prov. _____ Zip/Postal Code _____

Signature (if under 18, a parent or guardian must sign)

Mail to the **Silhouette Reader Service:**
IN U.S.A.: P.O. Box 1867, Buffalo, NY 14240-1867
IN CANADA: P.O. Box 609, Fort Erie, Ontario L2A 5X3

Not valid to current subscribers of Silhouette Nocturne books.

Want to try two free books from another line?
Call 1-800-873-8635 or visit www.morefreebooks.com.

* Terms and prices subject to change without notice. N.Y. residents add applicable sales tax. Canadian residents will be charged applicable provincial taxes and GST. Offer not valid in Quebec. This offer is limited to one order per household. All orders subject to approval. Credit or debit balances in a customer's account(s) may be offset by any other outstanding balance owed by or to the customer. Please allow 4 to 6 weeks for delivery. Offer available while quantities last.

Your Privacy: Silhouette is committed to protecting your privacy. Our Privacy Policy is available online at www.eHarlequin.com or upon request from the Reader Service. From time to time we make our lists of customers available to reputable third parties who may have a product or service of interest to you. If you would prefer we not share your name and address, please check here. ☐

SN08R

nocturne™

COMING NEXT MONTH

#49 AFTERSHOCK • Sharon Sala, Janis Reams Hudson, Debra Cowan

Don't miss these captivating tales of how life-threatening accidents vest three ordinary women with extraordinary powers. In "Penance," a gunshot wound provides Nicole Masters with the unusual ability to tune in to people in jeopardy. Now she and her boyfriend, Detective Dominic Tucci, team up to rescue an innocent child before time runs out.

In "After the Lightning," Hailey Cameron starts hearing voices in her head after being struck by lightning. Can former police detective Aaron Trent now help her channel this ability to stop an underground child-smuggling ring?

And in "Seeing Red," a near-death experience has firefighter Cass Holister witnessing fires before they happen. But it's proving harder to deal with Ben Wyrick, who is investigating the blazes, than it is to handle her new talent....

#50 VEILED TRUTH • Vivi Anna
The Valorian Chronicles

Not even her skills as a witch can help one of Necropolis's best crime-scene investigators, Lyra Magice, solve a series of gruesome and bizarre murders. Who is behind these horrific crimes, and why? Then Lyra discovers an ancient text owned by dark witch Theron Lenoir. Lyra has every reason to dis-- Theron. But with the threat of a gateway to hell open--- imperative that the two find a common ground.